Something ghastly in the night . . .

Elizabeth followed her sister's gaze. There in the window was the palest, whitest, ghastliest face she had seen in her life. Not quite animal. But certainly not human.

"Oh—" she whispered, backing slowly away. The hideous apparition in the window was more horrible than any nightmare she'd ever had. "Run!" Elizabeth commanded, giving her sister a shove.

Slowly, the face opened what might have been a mouth, revealing cracked and broken teeth. Through the sound of Jessica's scream, Elizabeth could make out an evil-sounding laugh.

"I said run!" Elizabeth screamed again.

SWEET VALLEY TWINS

The Beast Is Watching You

Written by
Jamie Suzanne

Created by
FRANCINE PASCAL

BANTAM BOOKS
NEW YORK · TORONTO · LONDON · SYDNEY · AUCKLAND

THE BEAST IS WATCHING YOU
A BANTAM BOOK : 0 553 50341 3

Originally published in USA by Bantam Books

First publication in Great Britain

PRINTING HISTORY
Bantam edition published 1997

The trademarks "Sweet Valley" and "Sweet Valley Twins"
are owned by Francine Pascal and are used under license by
Bantam Books and Transworld Publishers Ltd.

Conceived by Francine Pascal

Produced by Daniel Weiss Associates, Inc,
33 West 17th Street, New York, NY 10011

Cover photo by Oliver Hunter

Bantam Books are published by Transworld Publishers Ltd,
61–63 Uxbridge Road, Ealing, London W5 5SA,
in Australia by Transworld Publishers (Australia) Pty Ltd,
15–25 Helles Avenue, Moorebank, NSW 2170,
and in New Zealand by Transworld Publishers (NZ) Ltd,
3 William Pickering Drive, Albany, Auckland.

Printed and bound in Great Britain by
Cox & Wyman Ltd, Reading, Berkshire.

To Leslie Walsh

One

◇

A girl stands on the widow's walk of the old Victorian mansion. Her hands clutch the rail. She scans the horizon, her eyes flashing with fury and hatred.

In the distance she sees two figures. Girls. Blond girls. Pretty blond girls.

The sight fills her with violent loathing. The girl watches them approach the front steps.

"I'll give you fair warning," she thinks. "Don't close your eyes in this house. . . ."

The two blond girls come closer.

"Don't close your eyes," the girl whispers. "If you do, you're mine . . ."

"Another day, another dollar," Elizabeth Wakefield said, trying to sound cheerful. She and her identical twin sister, Jessica, were walking to their baby-sitting job. For the last few weeks the twins and some of their friends had been regular baby-sitters for the five children in the Riccoli family.

Jessica nodded. "It's a good thing we're getting paid," she said. "More than a dollar too. Let's see, four dollars an hour for about five hours. That's about—"

"Twenty dollars," Elizabeth filled in. "But 'another day another twenty dollars' doesn't sound good."

As the twins turned a corner, Elizabeth could see the Riccoli house. The house was one of the oldest in Sweet Valley: a sprawling Victorian mansion with turrets, round shingles on the roof, and a widow's walk.

Seeing the house made Elizabeth feel even more uneasy. She half wished she could just forget about baby-sitting and go straight home instead.

Don't be silly, she told herself. *So a couple of spooky things have happened here when we've been baby-sitting. So what? There's probably a reasonable explanation.*

And Jessica's not worried about it. So why should I be?

"Hey, Elizabeth?" Jessica's voice broke into Elizabeth's thoughts.

Elizabeth glanced at her sister. "Yeah?"

Jessica took a deep breath. "Do you think any-thing—well—*spooky* is going to happen tonight?"

Elizabeth raised an eyebrow. "Don't tell me you're worried too!"

"Well—not exactly *worried*," Jessica said quickly. "I was just—kind of wondering." She flashed her sister a huge smile. "You know."

Elizabeth knew. "I guess you kind of have to

wonder. One of the kids has had a nightmare every single night we've been baby-sitting." She shivered.

"Every single night. You're right about that." Jessica nodded soberly. "But—that's not so weird, is it? I mean, we've had nightmares plenty of times." She made a face. "Like, everyone has nightmares. Right?"

Elizabeth considered. "Yeah. Everyone does." She wondered for a moment if everyone had nightmares that were as scary and vivid as the ones the Riccoli kids had been having. *But Jessica's right*, she told herself. *Everyone does have nightmares.* "Yeah," she said aloud, trying to sound confident. "Everyone has nightmares."

Jessica looked pleased. "And remember, the Riccolis just moved from Sacramento. They're in a new house, and their dad hasn't even moved here yet—"

"And their mom has to go out a few nights a week and teach a class," Elizabeth added. "Leaving them with baby-sitters they hardly even know! You're right. It all makes sense. Of course they'd have nightmares."

"Everything has a reasonable explanation, I bet," Jessica went on. They headed up the hill and stood by the front steps of the mansion.

Elizabeth looked up toward the widow's walk. She felt a sharp chill in the air. Suddenly, she remembered all the spooky things that had been happening at the Riccoli mansion—besides the kids' nightmares. The old gardener, Mr. Brangwen, who kept trying to the girls away from the house—and who had died in his sleep just a couple of days before. Seeing the secret room on the third floor, which was set up like a child's bedroom but covered with several inches of dust. Inside the room there was a photo of someone who bore an uncanny resemblance to the twins' own mother when she was twelve. The girl in the photo was named Alice too—their mother's name.

"How about the scratches on Juliana's back?" she asked doubtfully. In her mind's eye she could still see five-year-old Juliana waking up from a nightmare a few days ago, her back covered with angry red scratches.

"Well." Jessica cleared her throat. "She must have scratched herself."

"Really?" Elizabeth frowned. "Are you sure? Those scratches looked awfully deep to me." She shuddered. In her dream, Juliana had described a creature chasing her, a creature that had scratched her with sharp nails.

"They weren't *that* deep," Jessica said, fixing her sister with a look. "I mean, did you measure how far down they went or something?"

Elizabeth bit her lip. "Well, no, but—"

"I've scratched myself tons of times," Jessica broke in. "I mean, it's totally normal."

Elizabeth wished she could be as certain as her sister was. "But, Jessica—"

"Don't 'but Jessica' me," Jessica said impatiently. "You've scratched yourself before, and you didn't have a cow about it, did you?"

"No," Elizabeth admitted. "But wouldn't there be skin under her fingernails, then?" She screwed up her eyes, trying to picture Juliana's fingers. Had there been traces of her own skin, or maybe dried blood? "I mean—"

"How should I know if there was skin under her fingernails?" Jessica said loudly. "Come on, Lizzie, take my word for it. Juliana scratched herself. No big mystery."

Take your word for it? Elizabeth couldn't help smiling. She knew better than to take Jessica's word too seriously. Though she and her sister looked almost exactly alike, with long blond hair, blue-green eyes, and a dimple in their left cheeks, they were very different on the inside. Elizabeth was the more serious twin. She loved having long talks with friends, reading a good mystery, and writing for *The Sweet Valley Sixers*, the sixth-grade newspaper at Sweet Valley Middle School. Jessica, on the other hand, was much more interested in fashion, soap operas, and flashy ideas. And while Elizabeth valued precise and accurate reporting, Jessica sometimes twisted the facts around to suit her mood. But despite their differences, the sisters were the best of friends.

"No offense or anything, Jess," Elizabeth said, patting her sister's hand, "but I never take your word for anything if I can help it."

Jessica snorted. "That's why you're not rich and famous yet—hey, what's that noise?"

Elizabeth heard it too—a sort of scampering

noise from the porch. Ahead of her was a flash of black. For a split second she stood stock-still, her heart beating wildly. Then suddenly she realized what she was seeing. "The cat!" she exclaimed.

"The cat," Jessica repeated, wiping her forehead.

The Riccolis' big black-and-white cat stepped onto the porch and meowed loudly. A great load seemed to slide off Elizabeth's shoulders. "The scratches must have come from the cat!"

"You're right!" Jessica grinned broadly. "Of course it couldn't have been Juliana. She wouldn't be strong enough to scratch herself like that."

Elizabeth narrowed her eyes at her sister. "Whatever happened to 'take my word for it'?" she asked.

Jessica looked at her sister blankly. "Hmm?"

Elizabeth sighed and shook her head. *Typical Jessica*, she thought fondly, *changing her story to sound like she knows it all.*

Elizabeth eyed the cat as it stretched and purred. It looked gentle enough. But how could you be sure?

I don't much like the idea of baby-sitting a maniac cat, she thought nervously.

But she preferred a maniac cat to Juliana's nightmare monster.

Not that she'd ever believed in the monster, of course.

Elizabeth put her foot on the first step. She hesitated.

Nightmares aren't real, she told herself.

"Race you up to the porch!" she called over her shoulder at her sister.

* * *

"'Essica!"

Two-year-old Nate, the youngest of the Riccoli kids, greeted Jessica at the door with hand full of cat food. "For kitty!" he told her proudly.

Jessica took a step back. She liked Nate, but she knew better than to let him come near her with cat food. It would be all over her clothes in a matter of seconds. "Kitty is outside," she told him. "How about if we go put the cat food in its dish so that it's all set when it comes inside?"

"Kitty out," Nate repeated happily.

Jessica smiled. Spooky as the house could be, the Riccoli kids made it all worthwhile. *Well, the kids and the money make it all worthwhile,* she corrected herself. She looked around the living room. The furniture was pretty ugly, of course. Still, the room was bright and cheerful.

Ten-year-old Olivia was reading riddles to Juliana. Gretchen, who was seven, and Andrew, a year older, were rolling a tennis ball down the hallway that led to the kitchen. They'd set up blocks like bowling pins.

Of course there's nothing spooky about this house, Jessica thought as she led Nate to the cat dish in the kitchen. *How could there be, with so much going on?*

"Hasn't anybody seen my other shoe?" Mrs. Riccoli called out desperately. Limping a little, she came into the living room from the hallway that led back to the kitchen.

Elizabeth hid a smile. Mrs. Riccoli was always losing things. "Did you look under the couch?" she asked.

"Strike!" Andrew yelled from the hallway. There was the sound of blocks tumbling down.

"That makes me think of a joke," Juliana said loudly. "What lives in a zoo and likes to eat stew?"

"A monkey?" Elizabeth guessed, burrowing under the couch in search of the missing shoe.

"Nope." Juliana sounded pleased. "Guess again."

"An elephant?" Olivia suggested.

"Wrong!" Juliana announced triumphantly. "A *shoe*," she said. "Get it? A shoe lives in a zoo and likes to eat stew." She doubled over in hysterical laughter. "Get it? Get it?"

"That's stupid," Olivia said. "Shoes don't live in zoos."

"A shoe does live in a zoo," Juliana argued. "You can tell because they rhyme. Shoe. Zoo. Like that."

"So does Juliana live in a banana?" Olivia asked. She rumpled her sister's hair.

"Strike!" Gretchen yelled from the hall. Once again the blocks clattered to the floor.

"Where is my shoe?" Mrs. Riccoli shouted, a note of panic in her voice. She headed for the front door. "Andrew, Olivia, help!"

This is such a normal family, Elizabeth thought, wriggling out from beneath the couch. *They're busy and lively and happy. Of course the spooky things aren't real. How could they be?*

"If I don't get that shoe, everyone's going to be

grounded for twenty years!" Mrs. Riccoli shook her head, an amused smile on her lips.

Twenty years. Elizabeth's mind flashed back to the little secret room, covered with twenty years' worth of dust.

But Victorian houses are full of old hidden staircases and passages, she told herself, looking through the broom closet for Mrs. Riccoli's shoe. *Why not a hidden room too?*

Anyway, she thought, *the Riccolis are doing a lot of remodeling. They must know all about it.*

It all made sense. Jessica was right. Everything had a reasonable explanation.

"Did you say shoe?" Andrew appeared in the doorway. Something brown and shiny flashed in his hand.

"My shoe!" Mrs. Riccoli grabbed the shoe and shoved it on her foot. "Where was it?"

Andrew and Gretchen exchanged glances. "Um—well, we were using it for something," Gretchen said at last.

"Yeah, we only had nine blocks," Andrew explained. "So we kind of borrowed your shoe to use for one of the middle pins. It worked pretty cool."

Mrs. Riccoli shook her head. "At least I have it back," she said, darting quickly toward the door. "I was afraid I'd have to wear one of Nate's bunny slippers!"

"'Unny swippers?" Nate asked, puzzled.

"Bunny slippers!" Mrs. Riccoli swept Nate up in a big hug and kissed him, ignoring the traces of cat food still mushed into his hand. "Sleep tight! Have fun! Be good!" she cried over her shoulder as she stepped onto the porch.

"I hope you won't be late for class," Elizabeth said anxiously.

"Me too," Mrs. Riccoli said. "I'm teaching Romantic Literature tonight, and my students are always frightfully on time. But I suppose that's not something to complain about!" She was about to close the door, but then she stopped and peered into her purse, a look of dismay on her face.

"Now where in the world did you guys put my keys?" she asked.

Two

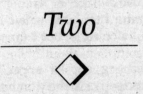

"So what do you guys want to do?" Elizabeth asked a few minutes later. Mrs. Riccoli had found her keys in Nate's toy garage, and the five kids were gathered on the couch around the twins.

"Bake a cake!" Andrew shouted.

"Play dress-up!" Gretchen suggested.

"Games!" Olivia put in, her eyes lighting up. "Checkers and Monopoly and Parcheesi and—"

"Cheesie!" Nate jumped up and down.

"Hold on, hold on!" Elizabeth held up her hand, laughing. "Just a few things, OK? You guys have to go to bed soon!"

"Boo," Andrew chanted, looking across at Juliana, who turned her face into a pout.

"No want bed," Nate announced.

"Yeah, can't we stay up just a little later? Just for tonight?" Olivia asked.

"Pleeeease?" Gretchen wheedled. Then Andrew joined in: "Pleeeease?"

Elizabeth was tempted to let the kids stay up a little late. *They're a lot easier to handle when they're awake,* she thought, remembering their bad dreams. *The later they go to bed, the less time for nightmares.*

"Well, an extra half hour won't hurt, I guess," Elizabeth said, catching Jessica's eyes.

"Add a heaping cup of sugar," Jessica read from the old recipe book she'd found in an out-of-the-way corner of the kitchen. She wiped her hands on her apron. "How much is a heaping cup, anyway?"

"A lot," Andrew told her. His eyes glinted, and he held his hand about a foot off the table. "Like, *this* much."

"More," Gretchen objected. "Like, *this* much." She held her hand a few inches above Andrew's.

Jessica made a face. "That might be more than we need," she said gently. "A cup is only this big." She showed the kids a measuring cup, and their faces fell. "Juliana, why don't you help me pour the sugar into the cup?"

Together they poured until the sugar was even with the rim.

"More," Gretchen said again. She made smacking noises.

"Gretchen's right," Andrew agreed. "That doesn't look like enough."

"It says a *heaping* cupful, remember?" Olivia reminded Jessica. "Heaping means, like, lots. We should pour some more."

"You can never have too much sugar in cake," Gretchen added as though she knew what Jessica was thinking.

"Make a mountain," Juliana whispered, not taking her eyes off the cupful of sugar. "A big white shiny mountain of sugar!"

Jessica shrugged. "Well, OK," she said with a grin. She poured sugar into the cup until it was overflowing. "But don't blame me if it tastes too sweet!"

"Too sweet?" Andrew asked innocently. "How could *anything* taste too sweet?"

"I'm gonna get you! I'm gonna get you!"

Elizabeth chased Nate down the long hall on the second floor, wiggling her fingers like a scary monster. Nate screamed with delight and ran in his bunny slippers, laughing so hard he could barely keep in a straight line.

"'Libabeff!" he shouted. "Go 'way!"

Elizabeth grinned and ran faster. "I'm gonna get you!" she yelled again, her footsteps echoing down the hall. "Run!"

Nate collapsed on the floor just ahead of her. With one quick motion Elizabeth scooped him up. "Got you!" she shouted triumphantly, and started to tickle him.

Nate giggled helplessly. He wriggled out of Elizabeth's arms and stood in front of her.

Elizabeth realized she was out of breath. "Do you

want to keep playing?" she asked. "Or do you want to rest a little first?" She stuck out her tongue and pretended to pant like a dog to show Nate what "rest" meant. But all she did was make Nate stick out his own tongue and dissolve into a new fit of giggles.

I must have been crazy not to want to come here to-night! Elizabeth thought, shaking her head.

"Four handfuls of chocolate?" Jessica stared at the page in front of her. "Huh?" *These old cookbooks sure are weird,* she thought. But the directions were clear enough. She turned to the kids in front of her.

"OK," she said. "Each of you take a handful of chocolate chips and toss them into the batter."

Olivia shook her head. "You should do it. Your hands are bigger than ours."

"Yeah," Andrew agreed. He grabbed Juliana's hand. "Look," he said, holding it up. "Four of *her* hands wouldn't be much chocolate at all. But four of *your* hands . . ." He paused and grinned up at Jessica.

Jessica grinned back. "I get it. You think there should be lots of chocolate in this cake, huh?"

Andrew nodded solemnly.

"And your hands aren't all that big either," Olivia went on. She pushed the chocolate toward Jessica. "Not compared to a grown-up. So maybe instead of four handfuls, you should put in—"

Jessica's eyes twinkled. "Five?" she asked mischievously, reaching for the bag.

"I was thinking six," Olivia said.

"Or maybe even seven," Andrew suggested.

With an even wider grin, Jessica did as she was told. After all, chocolate *was* one of her favorite things in the world.

"On your marks—get set—go!"

Gretchen and Juliana pounded side by side up the curving iron staircase that led from the living room to the second floor.

"When you get to the top, tag the upstairs banister," Elizabeth yelled after them. "Then come down and tag the next runner for your team!"

"Go, Juliana!" Andrew shouted.

"'Liana!" Nate echoed his big brother.

Jessica reached out and gave Nate a tickle. "You're on Gretchen's team, silly," she informed him. "Say 'Go, Gretchen!'"

"Go, 'Wetchen!" Nate yelled.

If we're lucky, they'll sure sleep well tonight! Elizabeth told herself, watching as Gretchen came clattering back down the stairs with a slight lead over her sister. She skidded the last couple of steps and tagged Nate on the head. "Go, Nate!" she yelled.

Nate threw his hands in the air and looked around proudly.

"Run, Nate!" Elizabeth urged him. She put a hand on his back and tried to push him gently toward the stairs. "Remember what you're supposed to do?"

Nate frowned. Then his face cleared. "Go, Wetchen!" he shouted happily.

Three

"All asleep," Jessica reported as she slid onto the couch next to Elizabeth later that evening. She put her head back and took a deep breath. "Boy, I'm beat."

Elizabeth stifled a yawn. "Me too," she said. "Baby-sitting is fun, but it sure takes a lot out of you."

Then her heart froze. Was it her imagination, or did the lights suddenly get dimmer?

Just my imagination, she decided.

Jessica squinted at the ceiling and frowned. "Did you get the cake stuff all cleaned up?" she asked.

"Oh, yeah," Elizabeth answered, trying to make her voice light. "It was good, wasn't it?"

"Well, if you like tons of chocolate," Jessica said dryly.

Elizabeth laughed a little too loudly. The sound echoed and re-echoed through the room. She bit her lip. Funny how she had never noticed how much the Riccolis' living room was like a cave.

Jessica wrinkled her nose and looked up at the ceiling again.

The room was so quiet, Elizabeth could almost hear herself think.

I really should say something, Elizabeth told herself, glancing at her sister. *Anything, just to fill the silence.* Now that the kids had all gone to bed, the big house seemed somehow emptier and lonelier.

And spookier.

I really should say something, she repeated in her mind. The silence loomed, almost like a third person there on the couch. But somehow she couldn't think of a thing to say.

Elizabeth's mind drifted back to Juliana's nightmare. The angry red scratches up and down the girl's back. The monster she'd dreamed about. The way the—

Whoa! Elizabeth shuddered, trying to shake away her scary thoughts. Juliana's monster was almost taking shape in her own mind. *It's only a dream,* she reminded herself. *And it's not even your own dream!*

Elizabeth rubbed her eyes. Next to her, Jessica sat on the couch, staring off into space. Elizabeth wished she could be cool and collected, like her sister. *How does she just sit there when—*

"Oh, my gosh!" Jessica shrieked all at once, pressing both hands to her chest.

"What is it?" Elizabeth asked with alarm, noticing the look of utter terror in her sister's eyes.

Slowly, the look faded. Jessica cleared her throat. "Nothing. I, um, thought for a second I saw . . . something."

"Something?" Elizabeth repeated, her stomach clenching.

"Um . . . a shadow or something. But I was wrong, see?" Jessica pointed to the wall. "Nothing at all." She laughed loudly.

Elizabeth gave a hollow laugh too. "Nothing at all."

Jessica glanced at the Riccolis' grandfather clock, which was ticking loudly in the quiet living room. nine forty-five. The kids had been asleep for forty-five minutes. *Not long enough,* she thought, watching the clock's hands move forward with incredible slowness. *One of the kids still could wake up with a—*

She didn't dare even think the word.

Was that a crying sound? With a start Jessica sat up straight and leaned forward.

"What is it?" Elizabeth turned to her sister in alarm.

Jessica hardly dared to breathe as she listened. She heard the ticking of the clock in the silent house. Outside, in the distance, a car driving slowly down the street. A dog barking somewhere down the block.

But no crying kids.

Breathing a sigh of relief, she settled back into her seat.

"Oh, nothing," she said carelessly.

This is crazy, Elizabeth thought. Every bone in her body felt tense. She almost wished one of the children would just go ahead and wake up with a—

With a you-know-what, she thought grimly.

At least that would get the suspense over with.

Taking a deep breath, Elizabeth turned to her sister. "Hey, Jessica?" she said gently, trying not to alarm her twin. "Maybe we should—you know, play a game or something while we wait."

Jessica frowned. "While we wait for what?"

"For—" Elizabeth swallowed hard. "For Mrs. Riccoli to come home," she said in a thin voice.

Jessica shrugged. "Sure," she said. "How about hangman? You go first."

"OK," Elizabeth agreed. She opened a notebook that Gretchen had left on the table and tried to think of a good word to have Jessica guess. *Nightmare,* she thought. *No.* She racked her brain for a less spooky word.

"Ready?" Jessica looked over her shoulder.

"Not yet." Elizabeth thought hard. *Monster,* she thought, giving a little shudder. *Nightmare. How about* evil? *No. Then* nightmare. She squeezed her eyelids shut tight. Little swirls of color danced in front of her eyes.

But she couldn't chase away the word "nightmare."

Elizabeth closed the notebook with a snap. "You know, I was thinking . . . hangman's pretty boring, isn't it? How about another slice of cake instead?"

*   *   *

Jessica sighed and ran her hand irritably through her hair. Having more cake had seemed like a good idea when Elizabeth suggested it. But now it was practically ten o'clock at night, the cake was gone, and there was nothing to do but wait— wait for someone upstairs to wake up screaming and sobbing.

In desperation she reached out and grabbed the riddle book that Olivia had been reading to Juliana. "Let's read some of these dopey riddles," she suggested. *Anything would be better than—waiting.*

"Riddles?" Elizabeth raised her eyebrows.

"Sure," Jessica said, opening the book at random. Normally she would have been embarrassed to read third-grade riddles aloud, but this wasn't normally. She glanced at the riddle in front of her. "What do you call a female horse who sleeps during the day?" she asked.

Elizabeth considered. "A female horse who sleeps during the day," she repeated thoughtfully. "Animals that sleep during the day are nocturnal," she said as if to herself. "A nocturn-horse?"

"You *wish*," Jessica said with a grin. "That doesn't make any sense. Give up?"

Elizabeth wrinkled her nose. "Give up."

Jessica turned the book upside down and checked the answer. With a snap of her wrist she slammed the book shut. "Nightmare," she said, laughing nervously. "Night mare, get it?" She tried hard to imagine a cute girl pony running through a moonlit meadow. But all she could think of was

Juliana waking up in the middle of the night, her body shivering with sobs.

Elizabeth made a face. "I get it," she said, "but I don't want to get it."

The twins exchanged looks. "You know what?" they said at the same moment.

Jessica smiled weakly. "I don't think these riddles are our kind of thing."

Elizabeth smiled weakly too. "Just what I was going to say."

"Jess?" Elizabeth checked the hands of the grandfather clock. It was almost 10:15. "Do you think it's been long enough for—you know?"

"Not quite." Jessica didn't meet Elizabeth's eyes. "Let's give it another couple of minutes, OK?"

"OK," Elizabeth agreed reluctantly. She looked around the room and shivered. "Is it cold in here, or is it just me?"

"It's just you," Jessica said a little too quickly.

Elizabeth burrowed deeper into the couch. She watched the second hand of the clock make two full circuits. It seemed to take hours. The house had never been so still—so ominous. She could feel the blood pulsing through her veins. She could almost hear herself breathing.

The second hand passed the twelve.

Elizabeth stood up. A sense of relief washed over her. *No way the kids will wake up now,* she thought. *Their nightmares always come less than an hour after they fall asleep.* "I guess we're OK," she said. Suddenly the room seemed warmer, brighter, more cheery.

Jessica stood up and stretched. "I guess you're right," she said. Her face broke into a grin. "So, how about it? You want to go explore the secret room some more?"

The secret room. Somehow Elizabeth's stomach suddenly felt jumpy again. She could see the room fresh in her mind. But more than that, she could see the picture—the black-and-white snapshot of two girls, Eva and Alice, Alice looking uncomfortably like their own mother, taken on the porch of the Riccoli house. *The Sullivan house,* she corrected herself, remembering that the house had belonged to a family named Sullivan long before the Riccolis bought it.

"No, thanks," Elizabeth said slowly. "Um—I'm just thinking about that picture. What if it's—it's—" She was almost afraid to say what she thought. Afraid speaking it aloud would somehow make it true. "If it's Mom," she said at last.

Jessica waved her hand carelessly. "Well, I have a theory about that," she said. "Listen. Who was that younger girl?"

Elizabeth frowned. "Probably the girl who lived here. The girl whose bedroom that was."

"Sure, that's obvious," Jessica said. "Her name was Eva. Eva Sullivan, I guess. Now, about that other girl—the one you thought was Mom."

Elizabeth bit her lip. "Well, so did you," she pointed out. "The girl's name was Alice, remember? And she looks like us, and like those pictures of Mom back when she was our age. And then there's the way Mom freaked out when she saw this house—"

"Calm down." Jessica raised a hand and leaned forward. "Don't *you* freak out on me now."

Elizabeth's heart was beating hard now. All her old fears had come tumbling back. Something was just plain weird about this house. Something spooky. Why else would there be a picture of her mother in a deserted bedroom?

"I'm sure it's not really Mom in the picture," Jessica said breezily. "Only a coincidence. There are lots of Alices running around. And just because it *looks* like Mom doesn't mean it *is*."

Elizabeth understood what Jessica was saying. Still, the whole thing seemed awfully mysterious. "Well, sure, but—"

"I bet that if we looked at that picture under a really good light, we'd be able to tell it's not Mom," Jessica said confidently.

Elizabeth wanted desperately to believe Jessica. *There has to be a reasonable explanation,* she reminded herself. "It *was* kind of dark in there," she agreed slowly. Had they taken the picture out of the dusty room? She didn't think so.

Jessica nodded emphatically. "That girl didn't really look that much like Mom when you think about it," she said with a wave of her hand. "She was too tall to be Mom, for one thing. Her hair was a shade or two lighter, and I bet Mom never owned a dress like *that*." She rolled her eyes. "I mean, no one with fashion sense *that* bad could grow up to be an interior decorator, you know?"

Elizabeth grinned a little despite herself. Maybe Jessica was right.

"We were just kind of freaked when we saw the picture, that's all," Jessica continued. "It would be a different story if we saw it again in the light."

After a moment, Elizabeth felt her jaw relax. "Maybe you're right," she said, smiling a little.

"Of course I'm right." Jessica propped her feet on the coffee table.

Elizabeth put her own feet up. *It would probably be easy to get that picture again and look at it under a good light. It would be easy to bring it down from the secret room. Even if the room is covered with dust.*

But she decided not to suggest doing that to Jessica.

"Well!" Jessica looked around at the living room and checked the grandfather clock. Almost ten-thirty. "Another day, another twenty dollars," she joked. She wished she could shake that spooky feeling about the house. The kids were in bed and all the weird stuff had a reasonable explanation. But she still felt—well—jumpy.

"Listen." Elizabeth held up her hand, a frown on her face.

"What?" Jessica held her breath. *Not another nightmare*, she found herself thinking. Hoping. Wishing.

A faint scratching sound met her ears.

"The cat?" Elizabeth asked. "It must be the cat." She hesitated. "Wanting to be let in. Right?"

"Yeah—probably," Jessica admitted. She squared her shoulders. *Of course it's the cat,* she told herself sternly. *There are no such things as spooks. Everything has a reasonable explanation. Everything.*

The scratching sound came again, louder and more insistent.

"It's coming from the front window," Elizabeth said. Jessica followed her gaze. "Don't cats—"

Elizabeth stopped in the middle of her sentence, but Jessica knew what she was about to say:

Don't cats scratch on doors when they want to be let in?

"We'd better check it out," Jessica whispered. "I mean," she added quickly, "we should let it in."

Elizabeth bit her lip. "We probably should." She laughed nervously. "Nothing to worry about. The cat's just used to coming in the window, that's all."

"Of course." Jessica tried hard to calm her pounding heart. "You first."

"No." Elizabeth clenched her fists. "We'll go look together. Just—just for, you know, company."

"Company," Jessica echoed. She grabbed her sister's hand, but she hung back as they walked toward the window.

Outside there was a howling noise.

Elizabeth stopped abruptly. "Do—do cats howl?" she asked, turning to Jessica. Her face was pale.

Jessica licked her lips. "I—I guess they must,"

she said, half to herself. She hoped with all her heart that this cat, at least, howled. Summoning her courage, Jessica stepped slowly to the window and pressed her nose up against the glass.

"Be careful," Elizabeth breathed behind her.

"I will," Jessica whispered back. She strained to see out. *At least it isn't one of the kids having a nightmare,* she thought. Somehow the thought wasn't very comforting. Jessica blinked. Stared. Blinked again.

What was that? A flash of sudden movement . . . something white . . .

A shadowy outline in the darkness . . .

Coming right at her!

Jessica couldn't help herself. She screamed.

Four

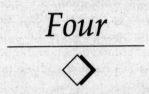

"What is it?" Elizabeth suppressed a scream of her own. Seizing Jessica's hand, she pulled her sister back from the window.

Jessica could only point.

Elizabeth followed her sister's gaze. There in the window was the palest, whitest, ghastliest face she had ever seen in her life. Not quite animal. But certainly not human.

"Oh—" she whispered, backing slowly away. The hideous apparition in the window was more horrible than any nightmare she'd ever had. "Run!" Elizabeth commanded, giving her sister a shove.

Slowly, the face opened what might have been a mouth, revealing cracked and broken teeth. Through the sound of Jessica's scream, Elizabeth could make out an evil-sounding laugh.

And she saw an angry red scar that ran from

one end of the white face to the other.

"I said run!" Elizabeth willed herself to look away from the monster. She covered her sister's eyes and dragged Jessica toward the living room door. "To the back of the house!" she called out frantically. A million thoughts whirled in her mind. How could they save the kids? Should they call the police? The fire department? Mrs. Riccoli? Their own mother?

"Don't let it get me!" Jessica gasped. She half ran, half fell into the dining room after Elizabeth.

Elizabeth tried to erase the image of the ghastly white face from her mind, but she couldn't. She thought of little Nate in his crib, and her heart thundered in her chest. The other kids could get out on their own, but Nate would need help. She made a dash for the kitchen. She'd have to run up and grab him . . . and then if one of the other kids was sleeping too soundly . . .

"Jessica!" she shouted. "I need help!"

"What?" Jessica stared up at her sister. Her eyes were frozen with fear, but at least she'd stopped screaming. Elizabeth made a quick decision. "Out the back door and hide!" she commanded. "I'll get the kids!"

She dashed back to the curving staircase in the living room. Up above she could hear the pattering of little feet and some cries.

Below her, Jessica let out another ear-piercing scream. Elizabeth turned around in alarm. Jessica was staring at the back window.

Elizabeth's blood froze. A second face, whiter and ghastlier than the first, stared in at the girls from outside. It had the blank expression of a zombie. As Elizabeth watched in horror, it opened its mouth and licked its red, red lips.

We're surrounded! Elizabeth thought. She'd never been so terrified in her life.

"'Libabeff!" Nate was screaming from upstairs, his voice squeaky and panicked. But Elizabeth couldn't move a muscle.

The face in the window leaned forward. Elizabeth could barely breathe. In its hand—*paw? Claw?* she wondered faintly—was a long, sharp knife.

A knife with a red stain at the end of the blade.

And Elizabeth began screaming too.

This can't be happening, Jessica thought, even as her screams echoed through the kitchen.

But it was.

Behind her, a door slammed. Crying loudly, Gretchen ran into her arms and held tight. The next moment, Andrew buried his head in her sweater. Jessica didn't want to look at the face in the window, but she couldn't seem to tear her eyes away. *I wish I'd never woken up this morning,* she thought, feeling the kids' shuddering sobs. *I wish I'd never come here at all! I wish I'd never heard of the Riccoli house!*

"What is it?" Olivia screamed somewhere across the room. Her voice sounded young and thin and terrified.

"Help!" Juliana sobbed. "Make it go away!"

"Don't look!" Jessica said, but the words stuck in her throat. She clutched Gretchen and Andrew tightly, realizing that she was trying to protect herself as much as them.

"Mommy . . . Mommy!" Nate's scared voice echoed through the mansion.

Jessica tried to focus her thoughts. "Call 911!" she cried, wondering whether emergency services could take care of gruesome monsters trying to break into haunted houses. But in the next moment she realized she couldn't remember where the Riccolis kept their telephone.

"How many of them are there?" she heard Juliana ask.

"Don't let them get me," Andrew begged, his body racked by violent gasps. "Don't!"

"Can we hide someplace?" Olivia asked, her eyes flicking back and forth across the kitchen.

The secret room! Jessica's heart leaped. *Of course!* They could hide in the secret room, and then the monsters wouldn't find them. "Come on," she shouted, moving toward the stairs. "Let's go to the—"

But then she stopped.

The back doorknob was turning before her eyes.

Elizabeth stood completely still while the door was pushed savagely open. *Don't—don't*, she begged in her mind, desperately wishing she'd locked the door.

A cruel laugh boomed across the room, and the first pale face appeared in the doorway. Elizabeth caught her breath. Up close it was ghastlier than ever. The broken teeth, the huge red scar, the almost luminous face. She'd never seen anything like it. Yet in the back of her mind she had the strangest feeling. A feeling that this figure was somehow familiar.

The second figure was close behind. Elizabeth gasped as her eyes traveled across the dead, staring, zombie face, down to the bloody knife, down to the—

The blue jeans.

Elizabeth snapped her head up. Suddenly she knew why the figures looked so familiar.

"Steven Wakefield!" she exclaimed, outraged. She had to look closely to be sure, but there was no question about it. Under the makeup of the "monster" in front of her she recognized the face of her older brother.

Steven slapped his arm against his leg and leaned against the door frame, laughing hysterically. "You—you—" He pointed a trembling finger at Elizabeth, then clapped the other zombie across the back. "Meet Joe."

Elizabeth put her hands on her hips and faced her brother and his best friend, Joe Howell. They were both clutching their stomachs and laughing like hyenas. She'd never felt so angry in her entire life. And her heart was still working double time. "Yeah, really funny," she snapped. "What exactly are you two trying to do, anyway?"

"Trying to scare you," Steven said, laughing helplessly. He hammered Joe on the back with his fists. "Guess it worked, huh? Wakefield and

Howell—" He choked for a moment but quickly recovered. "Wakefield and Howell, professional frightifiers! Whoa, baby!"

Elizabeth grit her teeth. "I can't even believe you guys!" she burst out. "I mean, do you just go around scaring little kids for the fun of it?"

As if on cue, Juliana began to cry louder than ever.

"You two kids don't look so little to me," Joe whooped.

"Yeah, it was you guys who screamed first," Steven added.

"She doesn't mean us and you know it," Jessica put in, her face turning red. "*We're* perfectly fine." She tossed her hair over her shoulder. Then she knelt by Juliana and gave her a big hug. "The question is, what were you *thinking*, scaring these kids?"

"We were *thinking* about giving you the fright of your lives," Steven gasped, practically sliding down to the floor in laughter.

"A real nightmare," Joe pitched in. "And it sure looks like we pulled it off!" He slapped his thigh and nearly fell over.

Elizabeth took a deep breath. She had to admit, the makeup was pretty realistic. Even knowing who the monsters really were, she didn't quite want to look either of the boys in the face.

Juliana whimpered against Jessica's shoulder.

"It's OK," Elizabeth said, reaching out to stroke the girl's hair. "Just a couple of clowns out past their bedtimes."

Jessica stood up, her jaw clenched. "Get out of

here and never come back!" she yelled, doubling her fists.

Steven gave her a mock salute. "Right away, sir!" he said in a squeaky voice. He scurried toward the door, with Joe right behind him.

But before he disappeared into the night, Steven turned around and grinned. "Hey, kids!" he shouted to the Riccoli kids, who had finally managed to calm down. "Aren't you happy that your baby-sitters are so incredibly brave?"

"Out!" Jessica yelled, running toward the door. It slammed in her face before she could grab her brother.

Elizabeth gathered the Riccoli kids close to her. "It's OK," she murmured. "It's going to be all right. Everybody back to bed—everybody—"

" 'Essica! 'Libabeff!"

Elizabeth bit her lip. Poor Nate! She'd forgotten all about him. "Coming!" she cried, clutching Andrew's hand.

"I can't go back to sleep again," Andrew murmured. "Not ever—"

"Me neither," Gretchen whimpered.

"It'll be OK," Elizabeth said soothingly. She forced a smile on her face and hoped she was right.

One thing's for sure, she thought as she climbed the wrought iron staircase to Nate's room.

I will never, ever forgive my stupid brother!

Five

◇

"You did *what?*"

Mrs. Wakefield put down the newspaper and stared wide-eyed at Steven. It was early Thursday morning, and the Wakefields were eating breakfast.

Steven shuffled his feet and grinned sheepishly. Not that he regretted his little joke last night. The expressions on the twins' faces had been totally awesome.

Too bad the girls had decided to rat on him. He had the sneaking suspicion that his parents weren't going to be what you'd call pleased. "Yeah, well," he said with a shrug, trying to buy some time.

Elizabeth calmly bit into a piece of toast. "Most of the time we wouldn't bother to come to you, Mom," she said, staring hard in Steven's direction. "But we felt this was pretty serious."

"I'll say." Mrs. Wakefield set down the paper and

glared at her son. "Of all the ridiculous things—" She shook her head, unable to finish her sentence.

"Thanks, Mom," Jessica said primly. She filled her cereal bowl with Corny-O's. "We knew we could count on you."

"I think you've got a lot of explaining to do," Mr. Wakefield informed Steven.

Steven realized that all eyes in the room were fastened on him. He laughed, aware that it sounded kind of feeble. "Can't you guys take a joke?" he demanded, looking from Jessica to Elizabeth and back.

"Some joke," Jessica said bitingly, eating a spoonful of cereal. "Seriously, Mom. It took us hours to get all the kids back into bed after Mr. Big Shot here decided to pull his little stunt."

"Juliana and Gretchen were sobbing nonstop," Elizabeth added.

"A joke," Steven argued. "A joke, right? J-O-K-E, joke. Ha ha, you know?" He took a sip of milk, then wiped his mouth with the back of his hand, trying to look carefree. "If the twins hadn't been screaming like they'd—they'd—" He searched his mind for a good comparison. "Like they'd broken a nail or something—"

Jessica shot him a withering glance. "I don't scream when I break my nails and you know it."

"Well, excuuuse me." Steven shoved back his chair and stood up. "Think I'll be heading over to school."

"Just a moment." Mr. Wakefield's voice halted Steven midstride.

Steven bit his lip. He didn't much like the look on his father's face. "Yeah, Dad?"

"First," Mr. Wakefield said, tapping the table with his forefinger, "you are to stay away from the girls while they are baby-sitting, is that clear?"

Steven felt his face redden slightly. "Sure, Dad. No problem." *I couldn't top that one if I tried, anyway,* he thought, but he was careful not to say it out loud.

Mr. Wakefield nodded gravely. "And second," he said, "you owe the girls an apology. A sincere apology, I might add."

An apology? Steven considered arguing. Normally he would rather die than apologize—especially to his sisters. And especially over something as completely unimportant as this.

"Steven!" Mr. Wakefield's voice held a warning.

Steven sighed. "Oh, OK," he agreed ungraciously. "Jessica, Elizabeth, it won't happen again. Promise. And I'm sorry."

I am sorry, he thought, the ghost of a smile playing across his face. *I'm sorry I got into trouble about it!*

"Obviously Steven has way too much time on his hands." Jessica sniffed. "Too bad he's not responsible enough to hold down a real job, like us."

"A job." Mr. Wakefield nodded firmly. "Excellent idea." He looked intently at Steven. "Think about getting a part-time job."

"A job? Me?" Steven put his hand over his heart in mock indignation. "Surely you jest."

Mr. Wakefield stood up. "Think it over," he said, clapping Steven on the shoulder. "And in the meantime, stay away from these two hardworking young ladies."

"Yeah," Jessica said. "The old Sullivan mansion is scary enough without Steven's help."

From the other end of the table Steven heard a sharp intake of breath. "Scary?" Mrs. Wakefield asked, in a voice that somehow didn't sound quite like her own.

Steven frowned. His mother sounded younger, somehow.

Mrs. Wakefield stared out across the breakfast table. "The Sullivan mansion—" She stopped short.

"Mom?" Steven asked tentatively, waving a hand in front of her eyes. Mrs. Wakefield didn't seem to notice. "Mom?" he said one more time, a little bit louder.

But Mrs. Wakefield just stared fixedly into space. . . .

Alice's evening with Eva had started off well. They'd played games in the old Victorian mansion. They'd read together. They'd brushed and braided Eva's long red hair. But when bedtime drew near, Alice began to feel nervous. She was only twelve, after all, and Eva was— well, a difficult child to baby-sit.

During the day young Eva was always a lot of fun. She was friendly, quiet, and polite—a lot like Alice herself. Alice felt that Eva didn't really belong in this big, forbidding house, with its spiral stairways, dim rooms, and long hallways. In Alice's opinion, the mansion would be perfect for a whole crowd of energetic kids, but not one thoughtful, lonely child like Eva.

"Bedtime, Eva," Alice said, ignoring the fluttering of her heart. She tried not to remember other evenings, other nights when Eva was left alone with her. . . .

Eva pouted. "Do I have to?"

Alice nodded, wishing she could let Eva stay up until her parents came home. Wishing she could let Eva lie on the living room couch, in the bright glow of the overhead lamp, until she fell asleep. Wishing that Eva could sleep peacefully and soundly, for once. "Yes," Alice said. "You have to."

Eva pouted again, but Alice managed to lead her to the spiral staircase. They climbed up to the third floor, to Eva's room. Eva called it her "secret" bedroom because it was so far out of the way. Alice could see the picture on Eva's bulletin board—the snapshot of herself and Eva together, smiling into the camera.

Alice closed the curtains over the glass door that led to Eva's balcony. Then she helped Eva into her favorite night-gown, the one with the little yellow daisies on the front.

"Can I wear my new bunny slippers tonight?" Eva asked.

Alice laughed. "Of course."

Eva slid the pink fuzzy slippers onto her feet. Gently she reached out and touched Alice on the cheek. "You have a hole, right here," she said in her soft little-girl voice, stroking with her fingers.

"That's called a dimple," Alice explained. "I get one in that cheek whenever I smile. See?" Quickly she moved her face back and forth from a smile to a frown. Eva smiled herself, watching the dimple come and go.

"You smile a lot," Eva said after a moment. "I wish I smiled more." Her eyes seemed heavy and sad.

"Oh, you smile a lot," Alice assured her, even though this wasn't true at all. She tucked Eva into bed and read her a story: **The Great Big Ball of String**, Eva's favorite. Then she gave the little girl her stuffed bear, kissed her good night, and switched off the light. "Sleep tight," she said softly.

Eva turned her face to the wall and pulled the covers up over her head. The bear lay on the pillow beside her. Alice could see the outline of Eva's bunny slippers beneath the blanket. Sleep tight, she thought again, hoping that this time Eva really would.

After a few minutes, Eva began to breathe deeply and evenly, and Alice knew that she was asleep. Alice began to leave the room, but first she locked the balcony door. She bit her lip as she checked it once, twice, three times. If she were to forget . . .

Downstairs again, Alice tried to do her homework in the ominously still house, but she had trouble concentrating. She huddled on the couch with all the living room lights on, listening. Listening for sounds of Eva.

Because at night Eva was a different child. Sometimes she would wake up sweating and crying, her sobs filling the entire house. Something in her dreams was disturbing her, she told Alice, but what that something was Eva wouldn't say and Alice couldn't guess.

Other nights Eva would walk in her sleep. So far, Alice had always been able to guide Eva back to bed, but she knew there were many dangers awaiting sleepwalking children. She shut her eyes, imagining Eva bumping *into a wall, Eva tripping over a toy, Eva stumbling into a dark closet. . . .*

She wondered whether she had remembered to lock the balcony door.

There was a faint sound in the hallway above. Alice snapped her head up. Eva! Too late, she saw Eva, eyes closed, poised on the very top of the spiral steps. Eva teetered on the edge, then reached out a foot, groped blindly in midair with her leg, and—

"Eva!" Alice cried. Springing into action, she dashed for the steps. There was a loud thud as Eva's body crashed against the railing. For Alice, time seemed to stand still. But curiously, there was no sound at all from Eva herself.

Alice frantically pounded up the steps, two at a time. She was grateful it was a spiral staircase; Eva couldn't possibly fall the whole distance at once.

Eva's leg bounced against the inner rail. She tumbled down the widest part of the steps, rolling faster—faster—

"Stop!" Alice commanded, knowing her words were useless. But now she was close enough to block the way. With a heart-wrenching thump, Eva's little body came to a halt against Alice's arm. Hands trembling, Alice helped Eva to her feet. Besides a few bruises, Eva seemed just fine. She was still breathing peacefully. Amazingly, she hadn't even woken up.

Alice took a deep breath. Slowly, she led Eva back up the stairs and tucked her into her bed. Then she carefully took off Eva's bunny slippers. No way Eva could be allowed to wear them to bed again, Alice thought. They muffled her footsteps, which was why Alice couldn't hear her walking down the halls in her sleep.

Still feeling faint, Alice stood up to leave the room. But first she walked once more to the balcony door. She knew she'd locked it. She was sure she'd locked it. She'd gone over it a dozen times in her mind.

Just in case, she reached out and jiggled the handle.

The door was locked. She'd known it would be.

So why was her hand shaking ever so slightly?

Six

"Phew!" Jessica breathed a sigh of relief as she sat on the living room couch next to Elizabeth. It was Wednesday, and the grandfather clock at the Riccoli house had just struck ten. "I guess we're home free."

Elizabeth nodded. "Not a single nightmare—so far, anyway." She reached out and tapped the wooden door frame next to her with her knuckles.

"I can't believe how well they all went to sleep," Jessica continued. She scooped up one of the cookies they'd baked that evening and bit in. "You'd think they were, like, different kids or something."

"I think it has to do with Steven," Elizabeth said. "Juliana and Gretchen were so relieved to hear that the monsters were just our wonderful brother and his best friend." She reached for a cookie too. "And they were especially glad when I told them Steven and Joe had been banned from this house. For the rest of their lives."

Jessica giggled. For a brief moment she wondered if Steven had somehow been responsible for everything that had happened. "Well, I hope the nightmares are over for good," she said. "You know, I'm actually beginning to like this house a little."

"Really?" Elizabeth ran her hand along the woodwork. "Well, me too, I guess," she confessed. "It may be big and kind of lonely at night, but it's got some beautiful stuff."

"If you get past the totally ugly living room furniture, that is." Jessica's eyes traveled up the wrought iron spiral staircase. "Wouldn't it be neat to live in a house with one of those?"

"The house would be perfect for Halloween too," Elizabeth added, her eyes shining.

"Totally awesome," Jessica agreed. In her mind, she started setting up the mansion for Halloween. Ten pumpkins on the porch—no, make that twelve, there's plenty of room. And a big old skeleton dangling from the widow's walk. "We could turn the dining room into a chamber of horrors," she said. "And shut off all the lights and roast marshmallows in the fireplace."

"Bats' wings," Elizabeth put in. "Eye of newt and toe of frog." She made her voice deep and spooky.

Jessica shivered with excitement. She almost wished the house actually were hers.

"And that little secret bedroom," she went on.

"We could make that into a mystery death trap. You know. One dark and stormy night, someone died here," she chanted. "Who? Why? How? Come inside and you too shall . . ."

Jessica's voice trailed off. She felt a sudden cold draft on her cheek.

Elizabeth looked at her sister. "Shall what?" she asked cautiously.

Jessica swallowed hard. A prickly feeling started in her legs and crept slowly up her body. "Uh, nothing. On second thought, maybe a Halloween party wouldn't be, you know, such a great idea."

Elizabeth shivered slightly. "Maybe not . . ." Suddenly she sat up a little straighter. "What was that?"

Jessica frowned. "What was what?" She listened intently.

"Ohhhhh—"

Jessica caught her breath. *A cry*, she thought. *One of the kids. Or maybe—*

Biting her lip, Jessica stared at her sister. "Steven?" she suggested hopefully.

Elizabeth shook her head. "One of the kids," she whispered.

"Ohhhhh!" The sound was louder. "Ohhhhh . . ." Then came a bloodcurdling scream. "Help!"

Jessica sucked in her breath as Elizabeth rose from the couch.

"It's Gretchen," Elizabeth said urgently. "Come on, let's go!"

*　　　*　　　*

"I—I don't want to talk about it," Gretchen said, staring fixedly at her pillows. She was wide awake now, but she wouldn't look the twins in the eye. "I'm a big girl. You can leave me alone. I can—take care of myself." She swallowed hard.

"Are you sure?" Jessica shook her head doubtfully. It had taken several minutes to get Gretchen calmed down, and her terrified screams had sounded as if she were in absolute agony. "Positive?"

"I'm sure." Gretchen bit her lip and took a deep breath. Looking up, she plastered a smile across her face. "See?"

Jessica hesitated. She longed to leave the bedroom and go downstairs, where she could huddle in a chair and watch the grandfather clock tick away the minutes until she could go back to the safety of her own home. But Gretchen didn't look ready to go back to sleep just yet. Jessica glanced at Elizabeth for help.

Elizabeth stroked Gretchen's hair. "You know, Gretchen, it helps to talk about the things that scare you. Especially when they're not real."

Gretchen sniffled and looked down at her hands.

"Little kids don't understand that," Elizabeth went on meaningfully. "They think if you talk about something, it must be real."

Jessica grinned. She saw what her sister was up to. "Like Juliana," she said. She gave a careless wave of her hand. "Juliana wouldn't know that. She's too little."

"But big kids do," Elizabeth said gently. "If you want to be a big kid and talk about it—well, we can help you."

Gretchen sat up a little straighter. She wiped her eyes on the sleeve of her nightgown. "All right," she said at last. "I was walking down the hall. You know, toward the stairs?" She made a curving motion with her hands.

Jessica nodded. "The spiral staircase," she said.

"But you weren't *really* walking there," Elizabeth pointed out. "It was just in your dream."

"Yes I was." Gretchen stared at Elizabeth as if daring her to disbelieve it. "It was real. A hundred percent real. A *thousand* percent real!"

Jessica sighed. *It won't hurt her for us to pretend to play along,* she thought. "All right," she said. "You were walking down the hall. Then what?"

"And I felt like—" Gretchen blinked rapidly. "I felt like someone was behind me."

"And then what?" Jessica pressed.

Gretchen shrugged. "That's all."

All? Jessica wrinkled her nose.

Elizabeth looked at Gretchen intently. "Some*one* was behind you—or some*thing?*"

Gretchen licked her lips again. "Something," she said, in a voice so small Jessica could barely hear it. "It was a girl. But it was also—you know. A monster."

Jessica stroked Gretchen's back. "You mean half-girl, half-monster?"

Gretchen shook her head. "At—at first it was just an ordinary girl. About my size. She had a nightgown on, like mine. It had little yellow flowers on the front."

"Daffodils?" Jessica suggested. "Or daisies?"

Gretchen shook her head. "I don't know. And she had a—" She gulped and closed her eyes for a minute. "A teddy bear. But then she—she—"

"She what?" Elizabeth prompted.

With a quick motion Gretchen rolled over and clutched the pillow with her free hand. "And then suddenly her face changed," she said in a burst of energy, "and she wasn't—you know—a person." Choking back a sob, she closed her eyes as if trying to shut out the image. "She was like a monster. She didn't have a face anymore. Just—flesh. Ugly flesh. Then she grabbed me."

Jessica waited for Gretchen to continue. "She grabbed you," she repeated.

Gretchen's nails dug into Jessica's wrist. "She grabbed me," she said again in a lifeless monotone. "And she tried to throw me down the stairs. And that's when—when I—when I woke up." A single tear trickled down her cheek.

"It's OK," Elizabeth said soothingly. "Juliana's nightmares have gotten us all a little jumpy. But you can see that it's not real." Her voice got louder and stronger. "See, I'm here. And so is Jessica. And Olivia's sleeping in her bed, and Andrew's asleep, and—"

"I know," Gretchen whispered. Her eyes darted anxiously around the room. "But sometimes—sometimes I forget."

"Well, it's no wonder," Jessica said. She was surprised to hear how loud and high-pitched her own voice was sounding. "Especially after what our stupid brother did a couple of nights ago. It's amazing that anyone can get any sleep around here."

"But it's not real, Gretchen," Elizabeth continued. "You see that, don't you?"

There was a sudden chill in the air. Jessica's stomach churned. *Of course it isn't real,* she thought. *How could a dream like that be real?*

Still—

It was an awfully big coincidence, two kids in the same family having dreams that were so much alike.

Jessica couldn't help wishing she were at home, where nobody had nightmares like these.

Where it was safe.

A girl stands in the old front bedroom of the mansion, watching with cold fury as the two blond girls try to calm the seven-year-old and her fears. The girl listens to the child tell about her dream.

She watches the exhausted child drift slowly back to sleep.

Her lips curve into a mocking smile.

I told you so, she thinks.

Don't say you weren't warned. . . .

Seven

"This is the life," Joe Howell sighed happily.

"You got it," Steven grunted in agreement. It was Saturday morning, and the boys were laying out by the Wakefield pool, munching on chips and dip. "Only one problem."

"What's that?" Joe raised his glass of iced tea.

"Ah, nothing much," Steven said. "It's just these shades." He held them out for Joe to inspect. "I mean, they don't even wrap around. I want those reflective kinds, with the mirrors on the lenses." He could see himself now, sitting on the beach with shades like that. The girls would flock toward him, that was for sure.

Joe grinned. "So buy 'em," he urged Steven. "You should have shades that, like, show what kind of a guy you are."

Steven stuffed a handful of chips into his mouth.

Then he turned up the volume on the radio on the deck beside him. "I don't have the cash," he admitted.

"Oh." Joe shook his head. "Being broke ain't no joke," he observed. "I know the feeling."

Steven wrinkled his nose. "My folks have been after me to get a job," he said in a tone that showed just what he thought of the idea. "They think I have too much time on my hands. What planet are they on?" he chuckled, stretching his toes and pouring more iced tea. It was amazing how often his parents failed to notice what a busy man he was.

"You too?" Joe sounded surprised. "My folks are the same way. It's 'get a job, get a job, get a job!'" he said in a high-pitched voice. "And I'm like, 'Get a life, guys!'" He shook his head in bewilderment. "I've got things to do, know what I mean?"

Steven knew. "Maybe we ought to go into business together," he suggested sarcastically.

Joe sat up straighter. "Hey. Maybe we should," he said slowly.

Steven frowned at his friend. "You're joking—right?" He could imagine nothing worse than having to give up—well—*this*. Lounging around the pool while everybody else was hard at work. "You're not suggesting we start our own *baby-sitting* service, are you?" he asked, his voice oozing with disdain. "Or maybe we could walk people's *dogs* or something." He thought back to a book he'd seen once at the public library: *Dog Walking for Fun and Profit*. "You sure you're feeling OK?" he asked.

Joe waved his hand in the air. "Not baby-sitting

or anything dumb like that," he assured Steven. "No. I was thinking of something—interesting. Something using brainpower, know what I mean?" He tapped his forehead. "Like inventing a machine. You know. Something like that. Exercise equipment, say."

"Or high-tech stuff," Steven suggested, starting to get the idea. "Fixing computers."

"*Building* computers." Joe spread out his hands grandly. "Or designing them."

"You can make a mint doing that," Steven said, sitting up straighter himself. "I read about it in a magazine. They pay you, like, thousands of dollars an hour."

"Thousands?" Joe's eyebrows shot up.

"Sure, thousands," Steven told him, wondering if that might be a slight exaggeration. He swung his legs around the end of his chair. "I wonder if we could do that. I mean, even if we only made a couple hundred bucks an hour it would be pretty decent."

Joe nodded knowingly. "You could buy a lot of shades with that kind of cash."

"You sure could," Steven agreed. Now he was really beginning to get excited. "I know it's hard to get a business up and running, but my mom could give us some pointers."

"We'd probably have to get permits," Joe said. "And licenses."

"No problemo," Steven said with a sweep of his arm. He decided they would need a big office—preferably with a plush carpet and a really snazzy telephone system—and two or three workers at their beck and call. No, make that *lots* of workers at their beck and call. A couple dozen at least. And he and Joe would wander in from time to time to fire a few people and put their feet up on the desks and return calls to their clients, who would always be respectful and would never *think* of calling them dorks or dweebs, unlike *some* people he could mention. . . .

Joe frowned. "Of course," he said slowly, "there *is* one minor detail."

"Which is?" Steven asked, barely listening. *Or maybe we could just take all our calls here at the pool,* he thought dreamily.

"Neither of us is exactly an expert on computers," Joe pointed out, running his hand through his hair.

"Huh?" Steven looked up, startled. "I took a programming class once."

Joe just shook his head. "Did they teach you how to make your own Web page?" he asked.

"My own what?" Steven asked.

"I rest my case." Joe spread out his arms.

Bummer. Steven hated to admit it, but Joe had a point. If you were going to make big bucks designing computers, it helped to know what you were doing. He looked down at the ground and made a face. It was hard being so close to a million dollars—and yet so far.

"I still think scaring people is our best bet," Joe said a few minutes later. The boys were floating on rafts in the deep end of the pool.

Steven grinned and spouted a stream of water toward the deck. "We sure do that well, don't we?" he asked. "Too bad nobody but us appreciated that joke we played on the twins."

"Yeah, it was totally awesome," Joe said with enthusiasm. He paddled his raft to the side and pushed off. "I think we should never have walked in the door. We should have just, you know, slunk off into the night. Like, *bam!*" He made a fist and splashed it into the water. "Two horrible monsters, there one minute, gone the next." Laughing loudly, he leaned back as far as he could. "Your sisters would never have known what hit them."

"No way!" Steven shook his head. "Why do a prank if you don't even get credit for it? It's not much of a joke if the victims don't even know they've been joked."

"Joked?" Joe frowned.

"Tricked. Fooled. Whatever." Steven waved his hand in the air. "You know what I mean." As far as he was concerned, the prank just wouldn't have been as good if his sisters hadn't known whose mighty brain was responsible.

Joe backpaddled so his raft was right next to Steven's. "So you're saying that practical jokers ought to admit it?" he asked.

Wasn't it obvious? "Yeah," Steven said belligerently. "You want to make something of it?"

Joe shook his head. Then, like lightning, his arm flew out. The next thing Steven knew, he was turning head over heels, his cheap sunglasses glinting in the sunlight. "Hey!" he yelled.

The shades tumbled off. The edge of the raft blotted out the sun altogether. Holding his breath, Steven slammed full force through the water and down toward the bottom.

Just wait till I get that Howell! Angrily he swam for the surface, kicking violently through the water. Ahead of him he could see Joe's raft floating innocently, a patch of red against the deep blue sky. *Hi-yaah!* he thought, using his best karate move against the raft.

Oops. Too late, Steven realized that no one was on his raft at all. Joe was sitting calmly on the edge of the deck.

Treading water, Steven rubbed his eyes and drew in a breath of air. "Hey, Howell!" he shouted at his friend. "What's the big idea?"

Joe grinned. "Just in case you were wondering," he said casually. "The guy who played that practical joke on you? That was me."

"The look on your face," Joe chortled. He and Steven were drying off on the patio. "Radical!"

"Oh, knock it off," Steven told him, briskly toweling himself dry.

In the distance, a door slammed. "Hey, Steven?"

"Sounds like your dad," Joe said. His face spread into an enormous grin. "Go tell him what just happened to you."

Steven glared at him. "You want to live to be two?"

Mr. Wakefield appeared around the corner.

"Steven? I need your help. You too, Joe, if you can stay a few minutes."

Steven stared daggers at Joe. *You'd better,* he thought.

Joe swung his body up out of the deck chair. "Sure, Mr. Wakefield," he said, slipping on his shoes. "What's up?"

"I just need you to unload something for me," Mr. Wakefield explained. "It's in the back of the van."

Steven frowned. "What is it?" he asked curiously. He put on his own shoes and followed his father across the yard. His wet feet made little squishing noises inside his sneakers.

"A riding mower," Mr. Wakefield explained. "It was on sale, and I figured it was about time we got a new mower." He shrugged. Throwing open the back door of the van, he motioned to the humongous crate inside. "I had to take out practically all the seats to get it to fit," he said sheepishly. "But I hope it'll make mowing the lawn a little easier."

Joe studied the mower with a practiced eye. "You made a wise choice, Mr. Wakefield," he said.

"Oh, yeah?" Mr. Wakefield looked questioningly at Joe. "I didn't realize you knew much about riding mowers, Joe. Do you have one at home?"

"Nope," Joe admitted. "Never ridden one in my life. But I keep telling my dad we need one." He dug an elbow into Steven's ribs. "Now maybe he'll have to do some shopping, huh, Wakefield?" he asked.

But Steven scarcely heard. He was staring at the crate in front of him, dollar signs dancing in his head.

It might work, he thought with excitement. *It just might work!*

Steven gazed at the riding mower, now unpacked from its box and gleaming in the bright sunshine. He'd never seen a more vibrant, brilliant red.

It's not exactly high tech, he thought. *But so what?* He ached to touch the leather-covered steering wheel, to wrap his fingers around the gearshift, to lead the mower into a casual (but awesome) high-speed turn, preferably with wraparound shades on and some cute girls watching. . . .

"It's a beauty," Joe said.

I'll say, Steven said to himself. He cleared his throat. "Hey, Dad? When are you planning to—you know—start using this thing?" He tried to sound as nonchalant as possible.

Mr. Wakefield sighed. "Soon, I hope," he said. "But I really don't know. I'm kind of snowed under at work right now."

Steven snorted. "How long can it take to mow a lawn this size?"

"That's not the problem, Steven," Mr. Wakefield said. "It's the instructions." He reached into the glove box and pulled out a thick book. "I'm going to have to read this whole manual before I get started."

Steven grabbed the manual and began leafing through it. *Old people!* he thought. " 'Operating Instructions'; 'How to Start'; 'Care of the Engine,' " he muttered under his breath, reading the headings.

"'Disposal of Used Motor Oil'?" He frowned at his father.

"Used oil's a big environmental problem, Steven," Mr. Wakefield explained.

Steven sighed loudly and continued flipping through the manual. "'Caution'—'Caution'—'Caution'—," he said, reading the headings on the pages as he flipped. He could feel his eyes glazing over. "'Caution'—'Caution'—"

"Caution! Caution! Caution!" Joe chimed in, waving his arms around like a robot.

Steven shut the book. "A snap, Dad," he said breezily. "Tell you what. I'll get it up and running for you, if you want. I'll even mow your lawn for free—on one condition." He paused for effect. "That you let Howell and me use the mower for our business."

"Our what?" Joe's eyes widened. "We don't—"

Steven stepped on Joe's foot as hard as he could.

"Ow!" Joe screeched.

"You've been bugging me to get a job, Dad," Steven reminded his father, doing his best to ignore Joe, who was jumping up and down on one foot. "And this is it. Wakefield and Howell, professional quality mowing." Steven could see the newspaper ads now. "Wakefield and Howell. For all your landscaping needs." He winked ferociously at Joe.

Mr. Wakefield frowned. "Well—"

"Think about it," Steven insisted. "You'll get a beautifully mowed lawn, and it won't cost you a cent.

All you have to do is let us use the mower. What can go wrong?"

Joe raised his eyebrows. "You mean . . ." He pointed back and forth between himself and Steven. "Us?" he mouthed.

Steven swallowed a sigh and nodded irritably toward his friend. "Us," he mouthed back, wondering if he could replace Howell with somebody a little quicker on the uptake.

Mr. Wakefield rubbed his eyes tiredly. "You boys have some real plans for this business, I hope?"

"Oh, sure," Steven said confidently. "It isn't the kind of thing we thought of just yesterday, you know."

"That's true, anyway," Joe grumbled.

Steven shot him a warning look. He could already hear a radio spot in his mind. A businessman type saying, "My lawn was a jungle of weeds! Then I called Wakefield and Howell. Now life is perfect again." *Or—scratch that—maybe a really hot actress could read it. Or maybe—*

Steven's eyes lit up.

Maybe Johnny Buck. Steven pictured the famous rock star gushing about his business. And the next step would be infomercials on late night cable TV. "Oh, we've got lots of ideas," he said.

Mr. Wakefield stared at Steven fixedly for a moment. Then he let out all his breath. "All right," he agreed at last. "I guess it won't be a total disaster. Just read the manual before you start, OK?"

Yes! Steven was too thrilled to be offended by his father's less-than-perfect trust in him. "No problem," he said confidently, holding out his hand for the gas can and the ignition key.

"Our new business, huh?" Joe said after Mr. Wakefield had left. He put his hands on his hips and stared at Steven with admiration. "Got to hand it to you, Wakefield," he said. "You've got guts."

"Yeah, well," Steven said modestly. He filled the tank and screwed the cap on tight. In one motion he tossed the manual onto the pool deck and boosted himself into the driver's seat. "Hey, who needs to read the directions, anyway?" he asked cheerfully, groping for the emergency brake and releasing it.

There was a lurch. The machine began to roll downhill.

Steven peered down at the dashboard. A complicated array of levers, buttons, and dials stared back up at him. *Where's the brake?* he thought, reaching out and trying a couple of switches. Nothing happened.

Down here? Steven jiggled a few gears. The machine slowly picked up speed and bounced over a root.

A root? Steven thought with surprise. He looked up—

Wham! The mower rolled into the side of a tree and stopped.

Steven leaped off the seat and checked the front bumper. He heaved a sigh of relief. *Not a scratch*, he thought proudly.

"Don't need the instructions, huh?" Joe teased him, a broad grin on his face.

Steven swallowed hard. "Right," he said with a casual shrug. "I'm just, you know, checking out what this machine can do."

Eight

◇

Elizabeth gripped the arm of the Riccolis' living room couch, her whole body tense with anticipation. She was baby-sitting for the Riccolis on Saturday night, and she could think of a dozen things she'd rather be doing.

Beside her Todd Wilkins leafed idly through a magazine. Todd was Elizabeth's sort-of boyfriend and one of the kids who often baby-sat the Riccolis. "It's no good," he said at last, flashing Elizabeth a shy smile. "I keep almost getting interested in one of the articles, and then—" He shrugged. "And then I start thinking about—something else." His eyes raised ever so slightly to the ceiling.

"I know what you mean," Elizabeth confessed. "I wish—I wish—" She considered. "I wish Mr. and Mrs. Riccoli hadn't gone out tonight."

Mr. Riccoli had come down from Sacramento to

spend the weekend with his family. Late that afternoon he had called to see if the twins could baby-sit while he and his wife went to a movie together. Jessica had been nowhere in sight. Elizabeth had wanted to say no, but Mr. Riccoli had offered an extra dollar an hour to make up for such short notice—

And I never was much good at saying no to people, Elizabeth thought grimly, wishing she had just gone ahead and refused.

With another deep sigh she picked up Todd's magazine. "What's this called, anyway?" she asked.

Todd didn't answer. Instead he stared up at the ceiling, a thoughtful look on his face.

"Todd?" she said again, tapping him on the shoulder.

Todd sniffed the air.

"Elizabeth?" he asked with a gulp. "Do you smell smoke?"

"It's Andrew's room, I think," Elizabeth gasped. They pounded down the second-floor hallway, the burning smell growing stronger.

"He'd better be all right," Todd said anxiously. They skidded to a stop outside Andrew's door. *That's strange,* Elizabeth thought. She could have sworn she'd left Andrew's door open, which was how he liked it. But right now the door was shut.

"Andrew?" Todd called through the door.

There was no answer.

Elizabeth took a deep breath and coughed. The odor of smoke was unmistakable. "Open the door!"

she urged, covering her nose and trying to breathe through her mouth.

Todd's fingers fumbled for the handle. There was a loud click, and the door opened wide.

"Andrew!" Elizabeth darted into the room. She couldn't see any fire. And even in the darkness, she could tell right away that Andrew wasn't under his covers. She bit her lip as she surveyed the tangle of sheets and blankets at the foot of the bed. "Andrew?"

"Over there." Todd caught his breath, and Elizabeth turned to look. Andrew was standing in a corner, bent at the waist. His eyes were tightly shut. The fingers of one hand were stretched out, as if to push something away, and his face was frozen into a terrible cry—

But no sound came out of his mouth.

"He's asleep," Todd said softly. He seized Andrew's hand and dragged him toward the doorway. "Where's the fire, buddy?" he asked, trying to shake the boy awake.

Andrew didn't make a sound.

Elizabeth looked frantically around the room, searching for a wisp of smoke, some heat, a glowing edge to a paper. But there was no sign of anything burning.

"Andrew! Can you hear me?" Todd's voice was insistent.

Elizabeth yanked open Andrew's closet, half expecting to see a ball of flame shoot out from among the boy's clothes. *Not here*, she thought with relief. The Sacramento Kings pennant hanging above Andrew's bed wasn't on fire. Neither was the Johnny Buck poster on the opposite side of the room. Elizabeth pulled open the dresser drawers. *Not here, either. But then, where?*

She sniffed the air.

Nothing.

"That's strange," she muttered to herself.

The smell was gone.

"There was—there was this girl," Andrew said softly. He was finally awake and leaning weakly against Todd's shoulder. "I was walking down the hallway out there—" He pointed. "She—I could see her. Except I couldn't see her face."

Elizabeth shut her eyes. Andrew's dream sounded awfully familiar.

"Then she turned around, and I saw it," Andrew continued. He burrowed tighter against Todd. "But it wasn't a human face. It was, like, no face at all."

No face at all, Elizabeth thought with a shiver. *Just like Juliana's nightmares, and Gretchen's.*

"You just had a bad dream," Todd said gently, wrapping his arm around Andrew's shoulders. "Forget about it, kiddo."

But Elizabeth wasn't about to drop the subject. "And then what, Andrew?" she asked, almost afraid to hear the answer.

"And then—and then—" Andrew blinked back a tear.

"It's OK," Elizabeth said soothingly. "Did she try to push you down the stairs?"

Todd raised an eyebrow at Elizabeth. "What are you—"

"No," Andrew broke in, shaking his head. "She—she said she was going to set my room on fire."

Fire. Elizabeth thought back to the burning smell she and Todd had noticed.

Todd patted Andrew's back. "You were walking in your sleep," he said. "Maybe . . ." He frowned thoughtfully. "Maybe you were playing with matches."

"I was not!" Andrew burst out. "*She* was the one lighting matches." He gulped. "I mean, *it*. The—monster."

Todd opened his mouth, but Elizabeth laid a hand on his arm before he could say anything more. There was something she had to know—even if she dreaded hearing the answer. "What was she wearing, Andrew?" she asked.

Andrew took a deep breath. "A nightgown with flowers on it. Yellow flowers."

Elizabeth's heart sank. The same nightgown Gretchen had described.

"And—and bunny slippers," Andrew went on. "Pink ones. Only—" He screwed up his eyes as though trying to think. "But there was only one slipper."

"One slipper," Elizabeth repeated. She cast her mind back. Had Gretchen mentioned a slipper? She didn't think so.

"And she was carrying a teddy bear," Andrew went on. "It was so—so real. It was, like, in 3-D. I could smell the fire and see her—face that wasn't there, and—" He shook his head. "It wasn't a normal dream. Normal dreams aren't like that."

"Well, some are," Elizabeth said as firmly as she could manage. "Now go back to sleep." She spread the blankets up to Andrew's chin. "No more monsters tonight. I promise."

She stood up, motioning Todd to do the same and making a mental note to herself:

Ask Gretchen if the girl in her nightmare wore one pink bunny slipper too.

She hoped the answer would be no.

"We're home!" Mr. Riccoli announced as he and Mrs. Riccoli bustled in the door promptly at ten-thirty. "How'd it go?"

"Well—" Elizabeth frowned. On the one hand, she didn't want to talk about what had happened with Andrew at all. *If I go around telling people all these weird and unexplainable things,* she thought with a sigh, *they'll just sound even weirder and even less explainable.*

But on the other hand, she couldn't help hoping that there would be some kind of reasonable explanation. She glanced at Todd for support. "It was pretty smooth, but, well—"

"We smelled some smoke coming from Andrew's room," Todd said hurriedly. "Just a little while ago. He was sleepwalking and—"

"Oh, no!" Mr. Riccoli frowned worriedly. "I thought he'd grown out of that."

Mrs. Riccoli sighed as she slipped off her coat. "We should have told you earlier," she said. "But it was so long ago now, to be honest I'd forgotten all about it." She shook her head sadly.

"What?" Elizabeth asked.

"Andrew used to play with matches," Mr. Riccoli explained in a tired voice, sinking down to the couch. He stretched out his legs and kicked his shoes off. "Back when he was about four or five, he grabbed matchbooks whenever he found them and hid them around his room."

"Hey, just like I said." Todd nudged Elizabeth. "Playing with matches."

"But where did he get them from exactly?" Elizabeth wanted to know.

"Who knows?" Mr. Riccoli gave a hollow laugh. "Once he even brought a bunch to preschool. We heard about that, let me tell you!"

Elizabeth bit her lip. She wanted to believe there was a reasonable explanation for the burning smell, but somehow she wasn't certain. After all, Andrew was eight now. He'd stopped playing with matches years ago. Why would he suddenly start again?

"I guess the move has had more of an effect on him than we'd thought," Mrs. Riccoli murmured as though reading Elizabeth's mind.

Elizabeth's heart leaped. "You mean with all the stress—"

"That must be it." Mr. Riccoli sat up. "I'll have a

talk with Andrew in the morning. And we'll search his room. And—" He wiped his forehead. "And I'll move down here as soon as I possibly can, so we can be a family again. This has been so hard on all of us."

Of course, Elizabeth thought as she gathered her things together. *Andrew used to play with matches, and now that things are tough at home, he's started doing it again. He's re—what do you call it? When you go back to being younger.* It was on the tip of her tongue—

Regressed. That's it.

So the fire had an explanation. A logical, reasonable explanation. She was glad Todd had told the Riccolis what had happened.

And the nightmares had explanations too, she assured herself. Steven. The cat. Overactive imaginations. Mr. Riccoli being away.

Anyway, there was nothing to worry about.

That much was for sure.

Nine

"*This* is mowing the lawn?" Mr. Wakefield asked on Sunday morning. He let out a sigh of exasperation as he examined the yard. "Looks like a tornado hit it."

"Well—you know how it is." Steven shrugged, feeling faintly embarrassed. He scuffed his toe against a bare patch of earth. Was it his fault the riding mower had a control panel out of some science fiction movie?

"For instance," Mr. Wakefield continued irritably, pointing over to a scraggly place near a tree, "what happened there? It looks like you've cut the grass several different lengths at the same time."

Steven bit his lip. "That's sort of what happened, Dad," he said. "See, there's this stick that lets you change the height of the cutter? So you can give the lawn, like, a crew cut, or else you can make it all wild and springy?"

His father fixed him with a look. "Don't tell me. You were experimenting with it."

"Um—yeah," Steven admitted in a small voice. "But not to worry. I've got the hang of it now." He decided not to tell his father that he hadn't actually known what the stick was for at first. It had been set in the number one position, and he'd knocked it into the number five setting by accident. While trying to get it back to number one, he'd gone over and over the same area near the tree many times, working his way through settings four, three, and two in the process.

Nope, no reason to tell Dad the whole story.

"And here?" Mr. Wakefield indicated a section of grass near the garage. "Was this part of an experiment too?"

"Uh, you could say that," Steven replied. Mr. Wakefield was pointing to a ring where the grass was cut to practically nothing. But in the center of the ring the grass was high again. *Looks like a gigantic doughnut,* Steven thought, rolling his eyes. *Or an inner tube.* "That's where the mower got kind of, you know, stuck."

"Stuck?" Mr. Wakefield raised his eyebrows.

"Well, not stuck exactly," Steven said quickly. "Not *stuck* stuck. Just sort of stuck. I mean, the *steering wheel* got stuck," he added, halfway wishing that his family would tear out the grass and replace it with AstroTurf. "It locked. You know what I mean?"

"Locked?" Mr. Wakefield echoed. He looked blank.

"Yeah, locked," Steven said. "I was making a left turn, and it wouldn't go back." He made tugging motions with an imaginary steering wheel. "I just went around and around while I jiggled everything in sight trying to get it to turn the other way."

Mr. Wakefield sighed. "Didn't you read the instruction manual?" he demanded.

"Yeah," Steven said, knowing this was the exaggeration of the century. "Most of it, that is," he added with a shrug. "And instruction manuals are for losers, anyway."

Mr. Wakefield sighed again, louder this time. "Steven—"

"And I figured out the problem all by myself," Steven said hastily. He hopped aboard the mower. "See? There's a little button here that releases the wheel." He frowned at the control panel. Yep, that little button was there, all right.

Unless it was the little button next to it. Or the one next to that. Or—

Steven frowned again. There were more buttons on the dashboard than half a dozen people would need.

"And how long did it take to find it?" Mr. Wakefield went on.

"Oh, you mean the button?" Steven tried to laugh casually. "Not long," he said with a careless wave of the hand.

Way less than a year, at least, he added to himself.

And Dad doesn't need to hear how I used up practi-

*cally a whole tank of gas buzzing around before I finally
pressed this button—*

He hesitated. *Or maybe it was this one?*

"Well, thank goodness for small favors," Mr.
Wakefield said. "I have to go to the office. I'd really
appreciate it if the lawn could be mowed—all
over—by the time I get back."

"No problemo," Steven said, saluting smartly.
"I'll have it ready whenever you say, Dad." He felt
confident—and why not? By now he'd worked out
all the kinks. "I mean, *Captain* Dad."

"Just plain Dad is fine," Mr. Wakefield said, raising an eyebrow. "Read the instruction manual,
please, Captain Steven. That's how pilots get their
wings—and how drivers get their licenses," he
added meaningfully. "And one more thing."

"What's that?" Steven followed his father's gaze
as it swept once more around the yard—to the wild
and scraggly unmowed places, to the closely
cropped blades of grass barely sticking up from the
ground, to the crazily winding paths that Steven
had cut through the middle of the yard.

"Don't become a barber when you grow up,"
Mr. Wakefield said, clapping his son affectionately
on the shoulder.

"No way!" Joe stared across the mower at
Steven, his eyes flashing. Mr. Wakefield had just
left, and Joe was over to talk business. He put his
hands on his hips and draped one arm protec-
tively across the hood. "We're partners, right?

And I haven't had a chance to try it out yet."

Steven sighed. Joe could be such a pain some-times. Of course, he had to admit, his friend had a point. It wasn't much of a partnership if only one partner got to drive the mower. "All right," he said ungraciously, draping his own arm even more pro-tectively across the seat. "You can have a turn. A *short* turn." *And then I get it back,* he thought, won-dering if it would impress the chicks if he took the mower down to the beach and did some wheelies in the sand. "I need some more practice."

"Yeah, I can see that," Joe jeered, waving an arm at the badly cut lawn. "Like I could do worse! What are you trying to do—give your yard a Mohawk?"

Steven turned red. "It's harder than it looks," he told Joe. "I'd like to see you do better!"

"Easy!" Joe exulted, vaulting into the seat. "So what do I do?"

Steven sighed elabortately, then leaned forward. "Push this button, and then this one, and when they light up, turn this switch to 'Action,' and then—"

"Like this?" Joe interrupted. He pushed a few but-tons at random. The engine sprang suddenly to life. A cloud of acrid black smoke belched out the back end as the front end of the mower lurched forward.

"Look out!" Steven coughed, taking the smoke full in the face. "Wrong buttons!"

Joe didn't seem to hear. The mower headed to-ward the pool, the engine pounding as loud as a jackhammer. "You have to engage the clutch!"

Steven struggled to shout over the roar.

The mower picked up speed. Joe stood halfway up in his seat. Steven gasped as he heard a tearing sound. From under the racing mower appeared a shredded pair of in-line skates.

His in-line skates.

Steven felt like crying. One skate wheel spun lazily on the newly mowed grass. Another wheel had been sliced into two pieces by the whirling mower blade. The force of the mower had driven the top of one of the boots halfway into the ground. The rest of the boot was now a sea of purple confetti scattered around the yard, and as for the brakes on the back of the in-line skates—

At that moment, Joe let out a scream that was almost louder than the roar of the engine. Steven's heart lurched. The mower was barreling directly toward the pool!

"Put on the brakes!" he yelled, filling his lungs with air. Frantically he ran alongside the mower, amazed at how quickly it could go. "The brakes!" he shouted, careful to avoid the smoke pouring out of the tailpipe.

"Huh?" Joe turned in his seat and cupped his hand to his ear. "Can't hear you!"

Pop! A soccer ball belonging to one of the neighborhood kids was in front of the mower one moment—and in a zillion pieces the next. "The brakes!" Steven screeched. Terror-stricken, he judged the distance between Joe and the edge of the pool.

In his mind's eye he could see the mower churning across the pool deck, its shiny red front sliding out further, further, further, till the wheels were rotating on nothing but air. And then he imagined the mower starting to fall, plunging suddenly through the water and crashing to the bottom of the pool.

If Dad didn't like the way the lawn was cut, he thought miserably, *wait till he sees this! I'll be grounded for six months. A year. A century—*

"Brakes!" he screamed with all his might.

Joe stood tall in his seat and slammed his foot down. The mower skidded crazily toward the pool. The engine coughed violently. An extra thick cloud of smoke burst out of the back. Steven's heart was in his mouth. Would the mower stop in time?

Screech! The wheels careened onto the pool deck, running straight across a bottle of suntan lotion that Jessica had left out. The bottle burst and sprayed oil all over the underside of the machine. Steven watched in agony as Joe pumped the brakes once more. With an anguished hissing sound, the mower shivered and came to a sudden stop.

Steven heaved a sigh of relief. He felt weak all over. The front of the mower stuck about three inches over the side. *Another half a second, that's all it would have taken*, he thought, willing his heartbeat to return to normal. *The mower would've been six feet underwater.*

And I might as well have been six feet underground!

"You almost gave me a heart attack!" Steven

yelled to Joe. "Why'd it take you so long to put on the brakes?"

Joe stared down from the driver's seat. The engine coughed for the last time and died. "Braking is for losers," he informed Steven in a calm, steady voice.

"Oh, Steven." Mrs. Wakefield shook her head sadly. "Your in-line skates—the soccer ball—"

Steven wished his mother had waited to poke her head out the window until after they'd cleaned up the mess and backed the mower away from the pool. He took a deep breath. "Well—it's not really so bad, Mom," he said gamely.

"Not so bad?" Mrs. Wakefield stooped and picked up a piece of purple plastic. She fingered the jagged edge of the material and shuddered. "You don't think these can be put back together again, do you, Steven?"

A picture flashed into Steven's mind: himself and Joe, sitting at the dining room table with thirty thousand pieces of his skate and a bottle of Super Glue, painstakingly connecting all the shards together again. *It'd be the world's toughest jigsaw puzzle*, he thought. "No," he admitted aloud.

"These cost a lot of money," Mrs. Wakefield went on, staring at the broken skates in dismay.

Steven squirmed uncomfortably. He wished his mother wouldn't look quite so upset. "Well, I kind of needed a new pair, anyway," he said hopefully.

"And the soccer ball? And Jessica's suntan lotion?" Mrs. Wakefield shook her head helplessly. "Honestly, Steven!"

"Hey, they shouldn't have left their stuff lying around," Joe said, leaping to his friend's defense.

"Yeah," Steven agreed, nodding. "Jessica never puts anything away, you know. It's her own fault if—"

Mrs. Wakefield shook her head firmly. "When you left your baseball cards on the kitchen table last month, and Jessica spilled juice on your David Flynn rookie, whose fault was that?"

Steven felt his face redden. He realized that he'd been trapped. "I mean—well—that is—" *Oops.* "I still haven't replaced that Flynn card, you know," he grumbled, suspecting that at this rate it would be several years before he had the cash.

"And my herbs," Mrs. Wakefield went on mournfully.

"Herbs?" Steven didn't remember any herbs. "Are you sure that was, um, us?" he asked. "Maybe it was a dog or something," he added, hoping there was at least one crime he hadn't committed.

In response Mrs. Wakefield held up a few shreds of what had once been a wicker basket. "This looks more like the work of a mower than a dog."

"Oh. Um—yeah." Steven shuffled his feet. "Um—sorry."

"Sorry," Joe echoed.

"It was all Howell's fault," Steven said quickly. "I mean, mostly Howell's fault. If this guy would only take the time to read the stupid instruction manual—"

"What?" Joe asked incredulously. "It's your fault, Wakefield. If you'd just told me what stupid buttons to press—"

"I did too!" Steven burst out. "You just weren't listening, is all. And you should have braked when—"

"Steven!" Mrs. Wakefield stopped him with a look. "There's no reason to blame Joe."

Steven grimaced. "Well, I really am sorry about your herbs, Mom," he said in a small voice.

"I know you are, Steven. If only—" Mrs. Wakefield sighed again.

Steven wished people would stop sighing at him. In a way, it was almost worse when his parents acted disappointed with him, like this, than when they yelled and punished. *At least, when they punish you, it's over and done with,* he thought. Just now, he felt a little like a prisoner on trial waiting to see what the sentence would be. "If only what?" he asked cautiously.

"Nothing." Mrs. Wakefield rubbed her eyes. "Sometimes I wish you were a little more responsible, that's all."

A little more responsible! The words hit Steven like a ton of bricks. "What do you mean, I'm not responsible?" he demanded irritably. "I am too responsible!"

"You're responsible for breaking your in-line skates, anyway," Joe hissed in his ear.

Steven decided to ignore this comment. "I'm a very responsible person!" he exclaimed. "It isn't everyone who would work for hours trying to get a stupid lawn mower up and running! And if that isn't being responsible, I'd like to know what is!"

The thought flashed into his mind that it might have been even more responsible to have read the instruction manual first. But he pushed that idea back out of his brain.

"I mean, I'm *way* more responsible than Elizabeth and Jessica, for instance," Steven went on. "They're just messing up this baby-sitting business right and left."

"Oh, Steven," Mrs. Wakefield said softly. "I'm not comparing you to the girls. It's just—"

But Steven couldn't stop himself. "The girls blame all their problems on that old house," he said, working himself up into a fury. *If they can blame it on the house, I can darn well blame the mower!* "But that's not what's *really* going on. It isn't the spooky house, it's that they're immature, know what I mean, Mom?"

Mrs. Wakefield didn't say a word.

"Mom?" Steven waved a hand before her eyes. "Earth to Mom?"

But Mrs. Wakefield didn't seem to notice him. . . .

"Find the product of thirteen and thirty-nine. Show your work."

Alice wrote the numbers in her notebook. She was at the Sullivan house, trying to do her homework. But every little noise made her think of Eva, sleeping upstairs. She pushed her long blond hair out of her eyes and hunched over the assignment.

Had she locked the balcony door?

Three times nine is eighteen, I mean twenty-seven—*Mindlessly, Alice filled in the numbers. It was as though her body was solving the problem on its own—without even using her brain. She got the final result and shook her head. Thirteen times thirty-nine can't be in the millions! she thought, erasing. She shut her eyes to concentrate on her work.*

But she couldn't. She was painfully aware of the clock ticking behind her. Its echoes filled the room and assaulted her eardrums. With a growing sense of unease, Alice switched on the radio and adjusted the sound so it was low. She had insisted that Eva go to sleep without her bunny slippers tonight, but the little girl loved her slippers, and Alice couldn't be certain she wouldn't retrieve them from the closet. And that would mean that Alice wouldn't hear Eva's footsteps if she started walking in her sleep this evening.

Irritably, Alice tuned through several stations—country, classical, news, pop—without finding one that would calm her nerves. At last she gave up and snapped the radio off. She wished the Sullivans would come back early—

"Help me!"

The sound, faint and distant but chilling, was coming from Eva's room. At least she isn't sleepwalking tonight, Alice told herself, scurrying up the spiral staircase. As she entered Eva's room, she checked the balcony door from force of habit. Locked, of course.

"I'm here, sweetie!" she called out.

"Alice!" Eva whimpered. She was standing in the middle of her room, tears streaming down her face.

"Alice!" Eva's lips spread open into a look of unimaginable pain. "I'm so scared—"

"It's OK, honey," Alice whispered. Taking Eva's hand, she tried to guide her back to bed. It was surprisingly hard to do. Eva's muscles seemed to have gone all limp. She looked painfully thin as she stood there, shivering, in her nightgown.

Alice lifted Eva's legs and tucked them under the blanket. She could see the pink bunny slippers on the girl's feet. She shook her head, wishing the Sullivans had put them away. At least during the night. "I'm here, and your parents will be home soon," she said softly. "And nothing can get you. I won't let it." She repeated the old familiar words, rocking Eva gently back and forth, hoping the girl would soon go back to sleep.

"Alice?" Eva asked in a little wisp of a voice. "I-I—"

Alice leaned closer to listen. "What is it, honey?"

The words were muffled. "I-I-I'm scared."

Alice ruffled Eva's hair. "Of course. But it's only a dream."

"I know," Eva said, the words scarcely louder than a whisper. "I know that." But Alice wasn't sure she did. "I'm scared that—I'm scared I'm going to die in my dreams."

Alice shook her head. "You won't, Eva." For a moment she tried to imagine what it would be like to go to sleep every night thinking you might never wake up again. She shivered. The idea was too terrifying to think about. "That can't happen."

Eva's dark eyes locked with Alice's own blue ones. "Really?" she asked, reaching out to touch Alice's cheek in the darkness.

"Really," Alice assured her. "Even if you dream that you die, you are always still alive—no matter what," she added. "And you will always wake up again—no matter what."

Eva bit her lip and let her arm fall from Alice's face. "Even if—"

Alice waited.

"Even if it's a really bad dream?" Eva asked at last in an anguished voice. "I mean—really bad?"

How bad can a dream be? Alice wondered. But she only nodded, as firmly as she could. "No matter what," she repeated.

Eva hesitated. "Promise?" she asked. She reached for Alice's hand and clutched it with a strong grip, a grip that Alice found strangely unsettling.

"Promise," she answered, silently hoping she was right.

Ten

"Jessica?"

Jessica stroked Gretchen's forehead. "What is it, sweetie?" she asked, trying to sound as patient as possible.

It was well past Gretchen's bedtime on Monday night, and Jessica was exhausted. Todd had canceled at the last minute, leaving Jessica to manage the five kids all alone. *And not just putting them to bed either,* Jessica reminded herself. *Listening for nightmares, checking Andrew's room for matches . . .*

She rubbed her eyes. The evening had been long enough already, and it didn't help that Gretchen didn't look anywhere near ready to fall asleep.

"Would you stay a few more minutes?" Gretchen pleaded. She sat up in bed, huddled beneath the covers. "I'm a little scared."

Jessica wanted to say no. She looked around at

the bright and cheerful posters that decorated Gretchen's bedroom: a basket of fluffy kittens, a ship sailing on a moonlit ocean, a cartoon map of the world. *How could Gretchen be scared in this room?* she wondered. But it was obvious that the little girl *was* desperately afraid. *And if I leave now, Gretchen might never get to sleep.*

"All right," she agreed at last, flopping down on the twin bed next to Gretchen's. "I'll stay for a little bit longer. Just go to sleep quickly."

"I will." Gretchen pulled the covers up over her head and lay still. "Jessica?"

"Mmmm?" Jessica mumbled, suppressing a yawn. She hadn't realized how tired she was.

"Promise you won't leave till I'm asleep?" Gretchen asked anxiously.

"I promise," Jessica said. The truth was, she suddenly didn't feel like going anywhere. Going downstairs would take energy she didn't have. And the bed was awfully comfortable. "Go to sleep."

There was silence. But not the ominous, spooky silence that Jessica had grown to expect from the Riccoli house. Instead, this silence was restful, almost soothing. *Maybe it's just that I can't hear the grandfather clock up here*, Jessica thought, yawning for real this time. To keep alert she focused her eyes on the basket of kittens. *One, two, three*, she counted. *Four, five. Just like the Riccolis*. The thought made her smile.

Gretchen murmured and turned over in her bed. Jessica listened carefully. The girl's breathing was regular and even. *Good*, she thought. *Gretchen's asleep. That was easy.* But she made no move to stand up and go back downstairs.

I should do the rest of my homework, she thought drowsily. Her eyes drifted shut. With great effort she opened them again and peered at the kittens on the wall. *My homework.* She tried to make her legs reach out to the floor. But they wouldn't move.

Well, maybe it's OK if I wait just a few more minutes, Jessica told herself. *Just a few more minutes—*

Gently, slowly, her eyelids began to flutter. . . .

How much time had passed? Jessica wondered, walking through the darkened house. She ran her finger delicately along the hallway railing, feeling the familiar touch of the smooth curving wood.

Only—something was different. The wood felt almost *too* smooth. Too shiny. Too fresh.

The silence had changed too. Jessica had been lulled almost to sleep by the stillness just a few minutes before, but now the silence seemed to settle around her like a dark cloud. An ominous dark cloud.

She found herself wishing for noise. A lawn mower in the background, a car driving by with the radio blaring, someone to talk to. Anybody. Anything.

Jessica came to the end of the hall and blinked. There, in front of her, hung an unfamiliar painting—a blurry picture of lilies in a field.

"That's weird," she said aloud, her voice echoing through the narrow passage. There a different picture there last week, wasn't there?

Jessica frowned. In fact, now that she thought about it, she was almost sure she remembered another picture hanging in that very spot earlier that evening. Gently she reached out and touched the painting in front of her. Strange. It felt real enough.

She racked her brain, trying to visualize the picture she had seen there earlier. *Not lilies,* she decided. *Definitely not flowers, even. Not this painting. But—what?*

She couldn't remember.

Jessica glanced at the wallpaper. Vertical blue-and-white stripes, three wide ones, three narrow ones. That wasn't the wallpaper that had been there before, was it? Jessica was sure the Riccolis had plain yellow wallpaper in the second-floor hallway. She'd seen it thousands of times. Plain yellow.

Right?

Jessica reached for the door in front of her. *Mrs. Riccoli's study,* she thought. She'd only seen it once, but that was enough to tell it was about the messiest room on earth. It was even messier than Jessica's own bedroom. Books and papers had been strewn everywhere. *She drops scissors on the floor and leaves the vacuum cleaner turned upside down,* Jessica remembered. *Not to mention the coffee mugs that surround the computer . . .*

Jessica eased open the door and switched on the light.

The room was tidy. Organized. Straightened.

Jessica bit her lip. *Neat as a pin,* she thought uneasily. Where were the scissors? The papers? The coffee cups?

For that matter, where was the computer? A typewriter sat on the desk where the computer had been. The telephone suddenly had a dial instead of push buttons, and the answering machine had vanished—along with the three telephone directories that had been stacked on top of it.

This must be a dream, Jessica said to herself. She walked back to the hallway, closing the door to the study gently but firmly behind her. *It has to be!*

But what if it isn't? a small voice asked inside her head.

With a growing sense of alarm, Jessica walked up the stairs toward the third floor. Eva Sullivan's secret bedroom was at the top of the steps. Holding her breath, Jessica reached out her leg to step through the hole in the wall—

Only there was no hole.

Instead, there was a doorway.

Her breath catching in her throat, Jessica ran her eyes along the polished woodwork on the door. *Where did this come from?* she wondered. She distinctly remembered stepping through a hole in the plaster wall to get in before. *I know I did before*, she thought, fighting a sense of panic. *I know it!*

Jessica could hear the blood pounding through her temples. Feeling slightly dizzy, she pushed the door open and walked through into the room. It was different too. There was a small table lamp sitting next to the bed, the lightbulb burning brightly.

Jessica could smell the scent of fresh flowers. And the wooden furniture was polished and gleaming, without a speck of dust.

But strangest of all, across the room was a glass door. *I would have remembered a glass door,* Jessica told herself.

Wouldn't I?

Almost without knowing what she was doing, Jessica walked to the glass door and jiggled the handle. Locked. She pressed her nose to the panel and looked out. There was a small balcony: a balcony about three feet long with a low wall around it. A nice balcony. A great balcony for sunbathing on a beautiful day.

And yet it filled Jessica with dread.

Wake up! she urged herself. *If I'm really asleep, wake up!*

But she didn't wake up.

Instead, she whirled around as she heard a noise in the hallway. Footsteps. *Probably just one of the kids needing to use the bathroom,* she told herself. *Yes, that has to be it.*

She took one last look around the secret room— *Eva Sullivan's bedroom,* she added silently—and tried to edge toward the door.

But her feet wouldn't move.

The footsteps came closer. Jessica bit her lip. She could hear a strange swishing noise with every other step, as though she were hearing someone walking with one foot on a bare floor and the other foot muffled by a carpet. She pictured the hallway.

But there's no carpet out there at all, she thought.

The footsteps paused outside the door to the secret room.

Move! Jessica commanded herself, panic swirl-
ing through her body. She forced herself to take a
step forward. So she *could* move—but where could
she run? The door was out of the question. The
closet. *No; too obvious. The balcony, then.* She
turned—and stopped.

Something was in the room with her. She could
feel its presence. Slowly, unwillingly, Jessica turned
toward the doorway.

In front of her was the most hideous, ghastly
face she had seen in her entire life. The flesh was
yellowish black, hanging horribly off the skull in
places where it wasn't already decomposed. Jessica
longed to turn away, but somehow her eyes were
locked on the gruesome sight. Her eyes traveled
down the figure's body, which was crumpled and
battered. One arm swung loosely from its socket,
and one leg stuck out at a crazy angle. Bruises covered the hands. Jessica opened her mouth to
scream, but no sound came out. She reached for the
glass behind her.

The figure stepped into the full light of the
room. Now Jessica could see it clearly. *It's small*, she
thought. Her heart pounded wildly. *It's—it's a girl!*

Jessica's breath came in short gasps. Her eyes
traveled across the daisy-pattern nightgown
that covered the girl's ruined body. The teddy
bear clutched tightly in one mangled hand. The

single bunny slipper that concealed a foot.

The figure advanced another step. Jessica could dimly hear a faint hissing sound as it moved. All of a sudden, it reached out a bruised hand and grasped Jessica's sweater. With surprising strength for something so small, the creature pushed Jessica roughly against the balcony door.

No! Jessica cried. Once more, she couldn't hear the sound of her own voice. She put out a hand to steady herself and tried to dig her heels into the floor. *No!*

The hissing sound grew louder.

Behind her, Jessica could feel the weight of solid glass. She leaned against it, trying to push the monster away. *No*, she thought, shoving out the image of the terrible face, the dead-looking eyes, the flesh hanging in strips where the nose should have been—

There was a click.

Jessica felt the glass door swing slowly and silently open under her weight. She fought to maintain her balance. In her mind's eye she could see herself tumbling out the door and over the low railing of the balcony, down to the ground far below. Once more, she tried to scream.

The figure only pushed harder.

Summoning her last ounce of strength, Jessica kicked violently at the creature. The figure moved back for an instant, but just as Jessica started to straighten up, a long ghastly fingernail shot out and clawed at her sleeve.

"Let go!" Jessica's words seemed to catch in her

throat. She hung in the doorway, not inside, not outside, feeling the cool wind in her hair and trying not to think about the long drop to the ground below the balcony.

The fingernail clawed deeper. There was a sudden tearing noise as the fabric of Jessica's sleeve ripped, a sound that seemed to tear straight through her heart—

And then all at once Jessica was seeing Gretchen's frightened face. The room seemed to spin, and she sat up.

"Are you OK?" Gretchen asked anxiously.

Jessica looked around. No secret room. No glass door. She took a deep breath. No ghastly fingernails. No—monster.

It had seemed so real. But it was only a dream.

"I guess I was dreaming," Jessica said aloud, her voice soft and weak in the familiar bedroom. She gave Gretchen a thin smile and checked the pictures on the walls. The kittens, the ship, the map. Slowly she stood up. "Yeah, a dream," she said with more confidence than she felt.

"Just a dream?" Gretchen looked closely at Jessica's eyes.

Jessica didn't quite meet her gaze. *No reason to say it was a nightmare,* she thought. *No reason to scare her.*

"Just a dream," she repeated firmly.

"How was everything tonight?" Mrs. Riccoli looked anxiously at Jessica.

Jessica took a deep breath, not sure how to

begin. Nothing really *bad* had happened, at least not to any of the kids. It was just that the house gave her the creeps. But she didn't exactly know how to say that to Mrs. Riccoli. "Um, everything was OK."

"Really? I know the kids are having a tough time, poor things." Mrs Riccoli handed Jessica her money. "With me being out a lot and their dad going back to Sacramento—" She shook her head. "They're lucky to have baby-sitters like you and your sister. But they seemed fine to you?"

Jessica managed a smile. "Gretchen had a little trouble getting to sleep, that's all."

"Oh, well, if that's all!" Mrs. Riccoli seemed relieved. "No nightmares or anything?"

Just mine, Jessica thought. But she didn't see the point of mentioning that—just saying the words would scare Jessica all over again. "No," she said. She leaned down to pick up her backpack.

"Well, good night, dear," Mrs. Riccoli said, holding the door open for Jessica. "Thanks so much."

"You're welcome," Jessica said. She shouldered her backpack.

And at that moment she saw a huge angry tear down the sleeve of her sweater.

Eleven

This is ridiculous, Steven thought on Tuesday afternoon as he paged through the instruction manual for the lawn mower. *Totally ridiculous!*

It wasn't as though he had *meant* to run over his in-line skates, after all. Or Jessica's suntan lotion. Or his mother's herbs. And he'd cleaned it all up afterward, hadn't he? At least, the pieces that were big enough to find.

So what right did his parents have to keep him away from the mower until he knew the whole instruction manual by heart?

Steven's gaze flickered over to the mower. His father had backed the tractor away from the pool—without even asking for Steven's expert advice—and parked it against the neighbor's fence. "I could have done it, easy," Steven muttered to himself.

And how could anyone expect him to run a

mowing business when he wasn't even allowed to run the mower?

With a sigh, Steven plunked down onto the grass and read the first page of the manual. The first incredibly boring page.

Well, at least that's one down, he thought as he turned the page.

Only one hundred thirty-five more to go!

"You know, it was really weird," Jessica said thoughtfully. She and Elizabeth were in-line skating and the dream she'd had last night was still in her mind.

"What?" Elizabeth leaned into a turn and glanced over at her sister.

Jessica laughed carelessly. "Oh, nothing, really. Just that I had Gretchen's nightmare, I guess." She shot in front of Elizabeth, arms pumping hard.

"Gretchen's nightmare?" Elizabeth struggled to catch up. "What do you mean?"

"Well, it was just like what Gretchen told us," Jessica explained. "You remember. The girl without a face, the daisy-print nightgown, everything." Even in the daylight, the memory of the dream was awfully vivid.

"That *is* weird." Elizabeth frowned.

"I must have been listening too carefully," Jessica said. It was the only explanation she'd come up with that made any sense at all. "You know, the power of suggestion? She has the dream, I hear her tell about it, and then—bang, it's my dream too."

"I guess that would explain it," Elizabeth said doubtfully.

Jessica whizzed past Sweet Valley Crumb, the neighborhood bakery. "The only difference was what the monsters threatened to do," she went on. "Gretchen's monster tried to throw her down the stairs, but mine tried to push me out a window. Oh, that was another weird thing," she added. "I was dreaming about the secret room, only the secret room had a glass door and a balcony."

That was the part that really had Jessica wondering. If she dreamed her dream because she'd listened to Gretchen's, why wouldn't the dreams be exactly alike? She glanced at her sister, hoping Elizabeth would answer her question for her. After all, Elizabeth liked solving mysteries.

Elizabeth nodded slowly. "Actually, that does kind of make sense. Gretchen doesn't know about the secret room, but you do." She glided forward, arms outstretched. "And since you've been kind of wondering about the secret room—"

"Hey, yeah," Jessica said with excitement. "So maybe Gretchen's, like, scared of the hallway for some reason—" She stopped. Maybe "scared" was too strong. "She's thinking about the hallway, and I'm—thinking about the secret room," she went on. "Then her dream happens in the hallway, and mine—"

"Happens in a room that's been on your mind," Elizabeth finished for her.

"Yeah." Jessica smiled, beginning to relax.

"And you're sure the monster was the same as Gretchen's?" Elizabeth asked.

Jessica didn't want to think about the monster. "One pink bunny slipper and a teddy bear in her hand," she replied quickly. "Sound familiar?"

"Uh-huh." Elizabeth's voice sounded strained. "But, Jessica—" She swallowed hard. "Did you say bunny slippers?"

"*One* bunny slipper," Jessica corrected her.

Elizabeth was silent. Jessica swerved and took a quick look at her sister.

Suddenly, Elizabeth was looking pale—as pale as a ghost.

"Warning: Do not attempt to use this mower to cut anything other than grass!" Steven read with disgust.

"Like, I'm sure people use this all the time to chop up sidewalks," he said aloud. Leaning on his elbow, he kept reading.

"For instance," the manual continued, "do not use this mower to chop up a sidewalk."

Steven groaned. He didn't need to read all of this stuff! He was way smarter than the idiots they wrote instruction manuals for. He flipped to the next page.

After all, he reasoned, *Mom and Dad never actually said I had to read it. They just said I needed to know it. That's different. Hey, I already know half this stuff.*

"Caution," he read aloud. "To shift into reverse, first make certain you are seated properly on the mower."

"Whoop-de-do," Steven said, circling his index finger in the air. He could just see some poor slob standing next to the mower, saying "Duh—is this right?" and shifting it into reverse, and wham! the mower backing over his big toe. *Yeah, right.* Steven shook his head. *Not even Howell would be that dumb. Like, not even my sisters would be that dumb.*

Reverse.

Steven glanced over to the mower one more time. He'd need to put the mower into reverse to get it away from the fence, wouldn't he? Turning onto his back, he started reading about reverse gear.

"Warning: To back up this mower, it is first necessary to shift into reverse."

"Caution! Do not attempt to drive the tractor in reverse gear unless the engine is on."

"Extreme Danger!!! Do not attempt to use reverse gear when parked directly in front of a large stone wall!"

Steven made gagging noises. He looked down the lines of type to the diagram at the bottom of the page. "Shifting into Reverse," it said "Caution: Do Not Attempt This Maneuver Without Reading the Entire Instruction Manual First." The picture looked simple.

And the manual wasn't telling him anything he didn't already know.

Checking to see that his parents weren't watching, he ditched the manual and took a running start for the mower.

                    *   *   *

"One bunny slipper," Elizabeth repeated carefully as she and Jessica rounded a corner on their
in-line skates. "You're sure?"

Jessica rolled her eyes. "Sure I'm sure. It was
pink, and it had little ears. Just like Gretchen described in her dream."

"But she *didn't*." Biting her lip, Elizabeth slowed
her pace. Reluctantly, Jessica slowed down too.
"Gretchen didn't tell us about any bunny slipper. I
remember: Andrew was the one who mentioned it."

"What are you talking about?" Jessica demanded, trying to ignore the feeling of something
crawling up her back.

"*Andrew* told me about the bunny slipper,"
Elizabeth repeated. "The girl in his dream had one
on, just like the girl in your dream." She stared at
Jessica. "But Todd and I were baby-sitting that
night. You weren't there."

A cloud passed over the sun. Jessica glided
along, her head full of thoughts she didn't want to
be thinking.

"And Gretchen never said a word about a slipper," Elizabeth went on. "So—where did you get
the idea, then?"

Jessica licked her lips nervously. "Maybe Todd
told me," she said as dismissively as she could. The
wheels of her in-line skates dug into the pavement.
"Come on, I'll race you to the corner."

"Todd told you?" Elizabeth picked up speed.
"When?" she asked doubtfully.

I don't want to think about this, Jessica told herself. She flashed across the intersection near home. She didn't want to think about her torn sweater sleeve. She didn't even want to mention it to Elizabeth. She didn't want to think about her nightmare anymore. "Or—maybe Gretchen told me about it just before she went to sleep last night," she said. "Yeah. That's what happened."

"Are you sure?" Elizabeth didn't sound convinced.

"Sure I'm sure," Jessica said. "One bunny slipper. Pink. With ears. Right?" She leaned forward.

"Yeah," Elizabeth said hollowly. "But . . ."

Head down, Jessica pulled away from her sister and her ridiculous questions.

Funny, Steven thought. The gear shift in front of him looked a tiny bit different from the one in the manual. The thought made him slightly uneasy. But only slightly. He slid the key into the ignition and turned it. The engine coughed twice, then caught. The tractor sprang to life beneath him. *Perfect.*

"Now, let's see," Steven told himself. He pressed his hand onto the gear shift. "Push in." He did; the motor purred gently. Steven screwed up his eyes. *Pull up, right? Right.* Slowly he pulled the lever back up. The engine hummed a little louder. *Now slide the gear shift all the way over to the left.*

He slid the lever to the side. "Check!" Steven exclaimed happily. He released the lever.

Whoosh! The mower lurched forward at what felt

like a million miles an hour. Steven gripped the steering wheel, his eyes bulging with astonishment, a horrible sinking feeling in the pit of his stomach, as the neighbor's fence came closer and closer. . . .

Who cares where I heard about the slipper, anyway? Jessica thought. Her skates bit angrily into the sidewalk. She wished that she'd never told Elizabeth about her dream. No. She wished she'd never gone into so much detail. No. She wished—she wished—

I wish I hadn't dreamed about the bunny slipper, she thought mournfully. She tried to reason it out logically. *I didn't know about the slipper. Gretchen didn't mention it. But Andrew dreamed about it.* Which left a huge puzzle.

Try as Jessica might, she couldn't think of a way she could have known about the slipper unless—

Unless her dream had been real.

And she didn't want to think about that "unless."

Skates churning, Jessica sped through her driveway and into the backyard—just in time to see a flash of red leaping up at the neighbor's fence.

"Help!" a very familiar voice cried out.

"Steven!" Jessica screeched. She watched, transfixed, as the mower crashed into the fence. As if in slow motion, she saw Steven's mouth opening and closing. Frantically, he waved his arms. His body jerked backward. A small piece of metal flew off the front of the mower, and the wooden fence splintered into matchsticks before Jessica's astonished eyes.

"Help!" Steven screamed again. All at once, the mower was in the other yard. A yawning hole marked where the fence had been.

"What's going on, Jessica?" Elizabeth skated up the driveway, panting.

Jessica could only stare. The mower roared across the lawn. In two seconds the neighbor's rosebushes had become a heap of twigs and a few petals strewn across the grass. Jessica watched openmouthed as Steven stood up on the seat of the tractor, teetered, and jumped. He seemed to hang forever in space before falling with a thud to the ground. An instant later, the mower crashed into a tree. This time, it came to a shuddering stop. The engine coughed and died.

About ten feet away from Jessica, Steven sat up slowly. He rubbed his head and groaned.

"Are you all right?" Jessica asked, a tremble in her voice. She took a tentative step forward, forgetting she was wearing skates. "Are you—"

Steven swiveled his head. His eyes grew big as he caught sight of the girls. "Don't say a word!" he pleaded, his face white as a sheet. "Please! Not a single word!"

Mr. Wakefield grimaced. "Steven," he said softly, "what are we going to do with you?"

Steven took a deep breath. He cursed his rotten luck. The mower was OK. So was the tree. But the fence—well, the fence was going to cost him plenty. And when you threw in replacing the neighbor's rosebushes—how was he supposed to know they were *valuable* rosebushes, for crying out loud?

Steven gazed at the fence. Wakefield and Howell was going to start business in a pile of debt. He hoped Joe wouldn't mind too much.

Mr. Wakefield shook his head, a stern frown on his face. "You know, Steven, when I was your age . . ."

Lecture, lecture, lecture, Steven thought gloomily, barely listening. It occurred to him that it was a real shame to have had that accident so close to home. Since neither he nor Joe could drive a car, their customers would all have to live nearby.

". . . and when I wanted money, I earned it the old-fashioned way," Mr. Wakefield was saying.

By cutting people's lawns with fingernail clippers? Steven thought, but he didn't say it out loud. He still wondered why the mower hadn't gone into reverse the way it was supposed to. *Push in once, pull out, slide all the way to the left,* he recited, seeing a picture of the diagram in his mind. *And that was exactly what I did.*

". . . and even when I finally could afford that electronic calculator," Mr. Wakefield was saying, "and it cost fifty dollars and was as big as a shoebox and would only add, subtract, multiply, and divide, well, I don't mind telling you I read every *word* of the instructions before I even turned it on for the first time. . . ."

"Dad?" Steven gently touched his father's shoulder.

"I know your generation lacks that kind of patience," Mr. Wakefield said, "but I expect more from you. You see—"

"But, Dad." Steven pulled Mr. Wakefield's sleeve. "That's just it. I *read* the instruction manual."

Mr. Wakefield raised his eyebrows. "You what?"

"I *did* read the manual," Steven repeated. "Just like you told me to. I didn't touch the mower till I read all about getting into reverse. I checked the diagram and everything."

Mr. Wakefield searched Steven's face. Steven did his best to look sincere. "I don't get it, Dad," he said earnestly. "In, up, over to the left," he said in a singsong voice. "And it didn't go into reverse. Maybe the mower's bogus."

"Bogus?" Mr. Wakefield thumbed through the book to the correct page. "Tell me exactly what you did," he commanded.

"I pushed the gear shift in," Steven said, glad he remembered the drill by heart.

"Go on." Mr. Wakefield fixed Steven with a look.

"And then I pulled it up. And then I slid it over to the left," Steven said. "Just like it said in the manual."

He waited while his father's eyes flicked down the page with agonizing slowness.

"Hmm," Mr. Wakefield said at last. "Hmm!"

"See what I mean?" Steven demanded, leaning over his father's shoulder. He pointed to the diagram. "See?"

Mr. Wakefield's forefinger stabbed at a line just below the drawing. "Read this," he said.

"Caution," Steven read slowly. "Do Not Attempt This Maneuver Without Reading the Entire Instruction Manual First." He shook his head. "I *saw* that already, Dad."

"No, this one." Mr. Wakefield tapped the next line.

"You mean there was more?" Steven hadn't meant to say it, but now that the words were out of his mouth he decided to make the best of it. "Heh, heh. Just kidding, Dad." He wished he'd gone ahead and read that instruction too.

"Read it," Mr. Wakefield repeated firmly.

"All right, already!" Steven gave an elaborate shrug and leaned closer to the page. "Warning!" he read. "On most tractor models, reverse gear is reached by moving the lever as shown." He stared at his father. "So?" he asked belligerently.

"Keep going." Mr. Wakefield nodded meaningfully at the book.

"But on the RS–745," Steven read with a sinking heart, "ignore the above diagram. Moving the gear shift lever as shown will cause the RS–745 to suddenly leap forward at great speed."

Steven let the instruction book fall from his hands. Slowly he raised his eyes to the model number stenciled in white against the brilliant red paint of the mower.

RS–745.

"Oops," he said, baring his teeth in a sickly grin.

Twelve

"Gretchen?" Jessica asked. She leaned across Gretchen's pillow to stroke the girl's forehead. It was Wednesday night, and the kids had been listless all evening. *Maybe they're sick,* Jessica said to herself. But Gretchen didn't feel hot.

"Mmmm?" Gretchen sighed drowsily.

Jessica had been planning to ask Gretchen whether the monster in her dream had been wearing a bunny slipper, but she decided not to. *Why disturb her sleep?* she thought.

Especially since she was baby-sitting tonight with Winston Egbert. In her opinion, Winston was a completely hopeless baby-sitter. *He'd be no help if someone had a nightmare,* Jessica thought. That was for sure.

"What did you say?" Gretchen mumbled.

"Oh—nothing." Jessica gave Gretchen's hand a

squeeze. "Sweet—" She caught herself before she said "dreams." There wasn't any reason to give the kid ideas, was there? "Sleep tight," she said instead.

"Mmmm." Gretchen burrowed under the covers.

Jessica straightened the picture of a ship above Gretchen's bed and turned off the light. Gretchen's breathing was already slow and even. Jessica only hoped she'd *stay* asleep.

On her way downstairs, she checked the painting by the spiral steps. It looked like a city scene: buildings, people, and a park in the distance. She leaned closer to read the caption. Sacramento: the Capital of California, it read. Painted 1903.

No lilies. Not anywhere.

And the wallpaper that surrounded it was yellow.

Jessica stood at the top of the steps and listened. For no reason that she could put her finger on, she sensed a presence around her. As though something were living. Breathing. Moving.

Right there in the hallway.

"Hello?" she called softly.

Outside, she could hear the wind pick up strength. A car horn blared. A branch banged against the roof.

But inside, there was no answer.

Winston flung himself onto the living room couch and proudly raised his thumb in the air. "Juliana—down for the count," he boasted. "Nate—out like a light. And What's-his-face is in Slumber City."

"His name is Andrew." Jessica raised her eyebrows. If *Winston* had been able to get the kids in bed with no problems, something had to be wrong. "And they seemed OK to you?" she asked.

Winston gave an elaborate shrug. "No muss, no fuss, no bother. Boom!" He mimed a head hitting a pillow. "What's your beef?"

"Nothing, I guess," Jessica said slowly. "They just felt kind of quiet tonight. Know what I mean?"

"Quiet?" Winston hooted. "Like when I knocked over Juliana's ant farm?"

Jessica smiled. It *had* been a funny sight, Winston down on his hands and knees with Andrew, Gretchen, and Olivia, trying to put Juliana's precious ants back into their cage before they escaped into the walls and floors of the house. At the same time, Juliana was wailing uncontrollably, afraid that her ants were gone forever. And little Nate was busy squashing every ant he could find between his feet and chortling with delight every time he killed one.

"Yeah," she admitted, "but the kids still seem— kind of down tonight. Kind of quiet." What was the word on her last vocabulary test in English class? *Sub-sub something. Subdued, that was it.* "Subdued," she said aloud.

Winston smirked. "If these kids were sub-whatevered tonight, I'd hate to see them when they're hyper," he said.

Jessica just shrugged. "I've been here more than you, Winston," she said. "You're sure Nate's in bed OK?"

Winston wiggled his eyebrows. "I told him no candy till he's thirty-five if he didn't sleep."

Jessica smiled. Even when Winston tried to sound threatening, he only seemed ridiculous. "He probably laughed himself to sleep," she said.

"Hey, I resent that," Winston complained.

In the background, Jessica could hear the ticking of the grandfather clock. *Don't listen,* she told herself, remembering how the noise had spooked her other nights.

"Want to see a card trick?" Winston stumbled over the low coffee table.

"Um—not really, Winston." *Don't listen to the clock,* she told herself.

"You sure?" Winston pressed. "It's pretty cool."

Jessica shook her head. *Don't LIS-ten to the CLOCK—don't LIS-ten to the CLOCK—* She realized her thoughts were exactly in tune with the ticking of the clock. Maybe she needed a distraction—even a stupid one. "Well, all right," she told Winston.

With a flourish, Winston picked up a deck of cards and flipped through them, staring intently at their faces. "Ta-da!" he crowed at last, carefully picking two cards and holding them out to Jessica.

"That's it?" Jessica stared at the two cards in Winston's hand. One was the queen of spades, the other the jack of hearts. "That's a magic trick?"

"Of course not!" Winston sounded offended. He flipped the cards facedown. "Choose one. You know—pick a card, any card, and don't show it to me?"

Frowning, Jessica picked up one of the cards. *The jack of hearts.* "But—"

Winston dropped his remaining card on the table, faceup, peered at it carefully, and proceeded to cover his eyes. "Now the Great Winstoni will tell you the identity of your card. It is—it is—" He made mysterious swaying motions with his free hand. "It is the jack of hearts! Applause, applause, applause." He bowed deeply in all directions.

"Some magic trick that was," Jessica grumbled, letting the jack fall to the floor. "You only gave me two cards, and you could see the one I didn't pick."

"Does the lady doubt my magic powers?" Winston demanded, looking hurt. "The Great Winstoni is in touch with the spirits. In fact, some of his best friends are ghosts. In fact—"

"Shhh!" Jessica put a hand on Winston's arm. She could hear the light sound of a foot on the bare wood of the upstairs hallway floor.

It must be one of the kids, sleepwalking, Jessica told herself.

But what if it wasn't?

What if it was a girl without a face, wearing a single pink bunny slipper?

Jessica held her breath as the steps approached the spiral staircase. She didn't dare look up to see who—or what—it was. She sat, rigid, on the couch, her eyes fixed to a spot near—but not too near—the top of the stairs.

Next to her Winston gasped. "It's Gretchen!" He

sprang forward—and once again, tripped over the coffee table. Cards scattered across the floor, and Winston fell headlong against the couch.

But Jessica hardly noticed. A feeling of relief spread through her body. *Only Gretchen, sleepwalking. Not some monster girl. I can handle Gretchen.* But her relief quickly vanished. Out of the corner of her eye she could see Gretchen swaying from side to side as though listening to music from an invisible radio, her eyelids pressed shut, her arms at her sides, teetering, teetering on the top step.

Jessica had never moved so fast in her life. She ran toward the staircase, but before she could begin to climb, Gretchen fell—hard and fast and straight . . .

. . . And into the waiting arms of Winston, suddenly standing halfway up the steps!

"How did you do that?" Jessica gasped. To her utter astonishment, Gretchen seemed unhurt—and still sound asleep.

"You forget I am the Great Winstoni!" Winston exclaimed proudly. "I have magical powers and—and—"

He stared at Gretchen lying in his arms. His gaze flickered up to the top of the steps, then down to the bottom, as if measuring the distance. Turning white, Winston gulped and sank down on the step behind him, handing Gretchen off to Jessica in the process.

"Maybe we'd better just call it a lucky break," he said in the most subdued voice Jessica had ever heard from Winston Egbert.

*   *   *

"I think she's coming around," Winston said, staring at the crumpled form in Jessica's arms a minute later.

"Are you supposed to move someone when they've—you know?" Jessica asked. Her heart thumped wildly inside her chest. She felt as if it just might bounce right on out. What if Gretchen was in a coma or something? "Come on," she said anxiously, stroking Gretchen's cheeks. "Open your eyes!"

The girl's eyelids flickered. "Where—where am I?" she muttered. Her voice sounded thick.

"You're at home," Jessica said softly, breathing a sigh of relief. "And I'm here, and so is Winston, and—"

Gretchen's eyes focused on Jessica's own. A look of terror flashed suddenly across the girl's face.

"What?" Jessica asked urgently. "What is it?"

As suddenly as the look had appeared, it was gone. "Oh—" Gretchen's body went limp. Then she reached out for Jessica. "It's *you*," she said, her voice full of relief.

"And Winston," Winston added.

Jessica noticed a couple of small bruises on Gretchen's leg. *Boy, were you ever lucky*, she thought, shuddering at what might have happened. "Get some ice," she told Winston.

Winston saluted and dashed to the kitchen, tripping over the edge of the downstairs carpet as he went.

"What happened, Gretchen?" Jessica rocked the little girl slowly back and forth.

"She said—" Gretchen furrowed her brow. "She said—"

"Who?" Jessica whispered, though she suspected she already knew the answer.

"The monster," Gretchen blurted out.

"The monster," Jessica repeated, her stomach knotting. "The one with the bunny slipper?"

Gretchen's eyes widened. "How'd you know—" But instead of finishing her question, she began to cry—great heaving wails that shook her entire body.

"She said she'd come back for me and kill me," Gretchen said between sobs. "She said—she said—"

Jessica clung tighter to the little girl. "Tell me."

"She said she's going to kill us." It was obviously an effort for Gretchen to push out the words.

Wordlessly, Jessica stroked Gretchen's heaving back.

"All of us," Gretchen added in a voice just barely above a whisper.

"Oh, dear." Mrs. Riccoli leaned against the living room wall, a worried look on her face. "She *fell?* From up *there?*"

"But I caught her," Winston said, raising his hands over his head like a prizefighter.

"She's actually just fine, Mrs. Riccoli," Jessica added, pushing Winston aside impatiently. *That is, her body's just fine,* she added to herself. "That's why we didn't call you."

"She vas having a nightmare," Winston said in a

Dracula voice. "And she vas heading schlowly down ze hallvay ven—"

"She was sleepwalking, Mrs. Riccoli," Jessica put in quickly, wishing Winston would just shut up. "And unfortunately we didn't see her until she was at the top of the steps."

"Sleepwalking," Mrs. Riccoli repeated, shaking her head. "Oh, there I go again. I really should have warned you."

Jessica frowned. "What do you mean?"

"Gretchen has a history of sleepwalking," Mrs. Riccoli explained. She took off her shoes and wiggled her toes. "Every time something stressful happens in her life, she sleepwalks."

"Oh." A great load seemed to lift from Jessica's shoulders. That made sense.

"Well, it wasn't like we ever thought something *evil* was going on or anything," Winston said importantly. Jessica rolled her eyes.

"First day of kindergarten," Mrs. Riccoli said, chuckling. "She was up all night long, it seemed. Opening the refrigerator. Into Andrew's room. Walking back and forth on the couch. We'd take her back to bed, and poof!" She snapped her fingers. "She'd be up again in a minute."

Jessica grinned at the idea. "But she never—hurt herself?" she ventured timidly.

"She never has," Mrs. Riccoli said. "Now that she's bigger, though, I guess we'll have to be extra careful for a while. Maybe we'll even get one of those baby gates."

"That's a good idea," Jessica told her. After all, the important thing was that Gretchen was OK, and that she stay that way.

And Gretchen *was* basically OK. That was what Jessica tried to focus on as she shouldered her backpack. Not the dream about the monster-girl who wore one bunny slipper and wanted to kill them all.

Thirteen

◇

"Now all we've got to do is drum up business somehow," Steven said. He plucked a blade of grass from the lawn and stuck it idly in his mouth. It was Friday. He and Joe had spent the last hour shifting the mower into reverse. And out again.

"Yeah." A slow grin spread across Joe's face. "I know. We'll make a big sign." He traced a rectangle in the air. "Like, an ad. Then we'll drive the mower along the sidewalk through town, with the sign on the side."

"Hey, yeah!" Steven pumped his fist in the air. "Great idea, Joe."

"Hey, it was nothing," Joe said modestly. "Howell and Wakefield Landscaping OK with you?"

"Howell and Wakefield?" Steven glared at his friend. "In your dreams. We're calling it *Wakefield* and *Howell*. Whose mower is it, anyway?"

Joe's eyebrows shot up. "Who drove the mower through a fence?" he countered.

"Who almost drove *my* mower into the pool?" Steven argued, raising his own eyebrows a little higher than Joe's. "And anyway, you'd have done the same thing."

"A likely story," Joe scoffed. His eyebrows went up even further.

"Yes, very likely!" Steven didn't think he could raise his eyebrows any higher, so instead he half closed his eyes the way he had seen a really cool dude do in a movie once. "Wakefield and Howell, or I'm out of here."

"Tell you what," Joe said. "We'll play a little game of skill. First, I mow half your parents' lawn." Joe kicked the grass in front of him. "Then, you mow the other half. Whoever gets it done in the shortest time—"

"—gets to name the company," Steven finished for him. "OK, OK. Sounds good." He stuck out a forefinger toward Joe. "But no sabotaging the engine, got it?"

"Me?" Joe pointed innocently at his chest. "Why would I need to do a dirty trick like that?" he asked. "I'm sure to be tons better than you, anyway."

"As *if*," Steven said sarcastically, extending his hand to clinch the deal.

And making sure Joe wasn't hiding a monkey wrench in his palm at the same time.

"On your marks, get set, go!" Steven shouted. He pushed the button on his stopwatch. Tenths of seconds began to click by. *Faster, faster,* Steven urged the watch silently.

Joe put the mower into gear. With a roaring sound, the tractor lurched forward and sheared through the tall grass at the back of the yard. "How'm I doing?" Joe yelled, hanging a left.

"All right, I guess," Steven shouted back as noncommitally as possible. Actually, though he hated to admit it, Howell was pretty darn good. "You've got the right stuff, baby!" he squeaked, doubling up with laughter. *There.* Maybe Howell would look at him and crack up and fall off the tractor. . . .

But Joe just grinned and chugged around a flower bed. "Say what?" he called out over his shoulder.

"Oh, nothing," Steven sighed. He bit his lip. Joe guided the mower up to the fence and swung the wheel around to the right. *Maybe he'll hit a gopher hole,* Steven thought hopefully. To his dismay, a sign the size of a billboard flashed into his mind: Joe Howell Landscaping Service (oh, yeah—his friend Wakefield helps out a little too). *Maybe he'll break the axle. Or the transmission. And only I will be able to fix it. Yeah.* He concentrated on sending signals to the mower. *Break. Break. Break—*

As if in answer, the engine suddenly cut out. The tractor glided slowly to a stop next to a tree.

"What's the problem this time?" Joe glared from Steven to the tractor. "Didn't you put gas in this thing?"

Steven tried hard not to smirk. "There's plenty

of gas, Joe," he said, rolling his eyes. "You must have screwed it up royally, old buddy, old pal."

"Oh, shut up," Joe said. He straddled the front of the tractor and unscrewed the gas cap. "Number one, I don't believe you, number two, I didn't touch anything, and number three, this counts as a time-out." He stared into the tank.

"And is there gas?" Steven demanded.

"Yeah," Joe admitted. He replaced the cap and tightened it. "So what went wrong?"

Steven stopped the timer, sighing heavily. "I guess I'll have to take a look," he said. He examined the brakes, the shift lever, and the steering wheel. *Poor old Howell can't even figure out how to fix a simple problem like—*

Like—

Steven frowned. It wasn't the brakes, the shift lever, or the steering wheel.

"Got it figured out yet?" Joe leaned back, his voice heavy with sarcasm. "Or should I send out for pizza? From Seattle?"

"Oh, sure," Steven said airily. And suddenly, he saw the trouble. "Right here. You hit the emergency shutoff."

"The what?" Joe groaned. "What do I have to do?"

Steven looked virtuous. "You mean you haven't read the manual?" he asked, trying to sound as shocked as possible.

"Give me a break," Joe muttered. "Neither have you."

Steven sighed. Joe didn't need to know that

Steven had only discovered the shutoff switch by banging his knee against it several times. "Get off the hood," he said. "A serious mechanic has to take care of a serious problem like this."

"You?" Joe rolled his eyes.

And Joe doesn't need to know that you just move the switch back again to turn it on, he thought. *Time for a little razzle-dazzle here—*

"Wait a minute." Joe bent down suddenly.

"Watch it!" Steven yelled. He straightened up and lunged for the shutoff. But it was too late. Joe's foot had knocked the switch back to the On position. With a roar, the mower shot forward. Quickly, Steven swung himself into the driver's seat while Joe fell heavily onto the hood. "Hey!" Joe shouted, his fingers groping for a handhold. "Turn that thing off!"

Steven grabbed the switch and slid it to the Off position. But the mower picked up speed. The grass was a blur. Steven flipped the switch to On— to Off—back to On—back to Off.

Nothing.

"Help!" Joe shrieked, ducking his head as low as it would go.

Dimly, Steven remembered a line in the instruction manual. "Caution," he repeated to himself. "For safety reasons, the emergency shutoff may only be used once every ten minutes."

Every ten minutes? he thought. The blood drained from his face.

I'm going to be stuck on this tractor for the next ten minutes!

Quickly Steven took stock of the situation. He was at the wheel of a runaway mower. With his best friend sprawled across the hood in front of him. Making it impossible for him to see what lay ahead.

"Put on the brakes, you fool!" Joe shouted.

The brakes! Steven smacked the side of his forehead. How could he have been so dumb? *Put on the brakes,* Steven told himself, *and you're golden. Yeah.*

He reached for the brakes—only to find that Joe's dangling legs were in the way.

And as he frantically spun the steering wheel, he discovered that it had somehow gotten stuck in the left-turn position.

The mower careened around the west side of the house. Steven held on tight and did the only thing he could.

"Help!" he bawled.

"This makes twenty-three laps," Elizabeth murmured. Her face was pressed to the window of the family room, watching the tractor speed across the yard. Joe was twisted in an impossible position on the hood, screaming himself hoarse. Steven, meanwhile, sat rigid on the driver's seat, face frozen into a look of utter terror.

"Twenty-four," Jessica corrected her. "And they're going faster each time around."

Elizabeth shook her head as the mower disappeared around the side of the house. How had her brother gotten himself into this mess? "Shouldn't we do something?" she asked.

Jessica waved her hand dismissively in the air. "They'll run out of gas sooner or later. Hey, where's the video camera?"

"Oh, Jess." Elizabeth gave her sister a look of disapproval.

"No, really," Jessica said. "We could send it to that video show. You know, *The World's Stupidest People—On Tape!*" Outside, the mower chugged back into sight. Steven frantically tugged at the wheel while Joe paused for breath between screams. "Those two would definitely qualify."

Elizabeth rolled her eyes. The mower vanished again.

"We could have a contest to see how many laps they do before they run out of gas," Jessica added brightly. "I vote for three hundred and twelve."

Elizabeth couldn't help giggling. She watched as the mower rumbled back into sight. Only this time, something was different.

"Awesome!" Jessica whooped. "Now I *really* wish we had the camera."

The mower zoomed off again, but not before Elizabeth had caught her breath in astonishment.

Because now it was Joe at the steering wheel—

And *Steven* who was sprawled across the hood.

"I got it!" Joe cried.

Steven coughed violently as the wind blew tiny particles of dust deep into his lungs. The mower leaned awkwardly to one side. *I liked it better when I was driving*, he thought. "Got what?"

he managed to shout back through his coughs.

No answer.

The mower straightened out and made a beeline for the sidewalk. "Got *what?*" Steven shouted again, afraid he'd lose his balance if he turned around. It didn't feel as if Joe had found the brakes.

If anything, he'd found the accelerator. Steven winced. The mower leaped toward a parked car.

"I just jiggled the key!" Joe shouted happily. "It unlocked the steering wheel!"

The mower swerved to the right and then back to the left. Steven felt a scream rising in his throat. But before it could escape, the parked car had disappeared. "Find the brakes!" he shouted, hoping the wind would carry his words behind him.

"Brakes?" Joe repeated.

A little boy on a tricycle flashed into Steven's line of sight. "Left! Left! Left!" he shouted frantically.

The mower darted to the left. Steven held his breath, waiting for the crash. But there was none. Miraculously, the boy was gone.

"First you say brakes, then you say left!" Joe shouted angrily. "Make up your mind!"

"Put on the brakes!" Steven shouted.

"I can't!" Joe yelled. "Your legs are in the way!"

Steven tried to move his legs, but there was nowhere to put them. "I can't!" he cried.

"Then let go!" Joe commanded, yanking the steering wheel sharply to the right.

"Let *go?*" Steven repeated incredulously. "Are you crazy?"

"Down in front!" Joe yelled. "I can't see!"

Steven stretched out flat. He could see a busy intersection dead ahead. His heart sank. "Help!" he shouted.

"I still can't see!" Joe complained. The mower screeched across the road. Horns blared. Steven couldn't bear to look. He braced himself for the sound of breaking glass. *Or breaking bones*, he thought wildly, wondering how many bones you could break at a time and live to tell about it. "I can't go any lower!" he shrieked.

"Then take your head off!" Joe demanded.

The mower hit a curb and bounced up. Steven swallowed hard. He'd had no idea that mowers could go so fast. He held on for dear life as Joe maneuvered around a mailbox, past a barking dog, and through a freshly cemented square of sidewalk. *Get me out of here!* he thought desperately, his knuckles turning white.

There was an ominous crunch. But the mower didn't even slow down. "What was that?" Steven squealed.

"A For Sale sign!" Joe told him.

Steven ducked his head down and held tight. A million thoughts whirled through his mind, including a heartfelt, absolutely sincere promise:

If he ever got out of this one alive, he would donate his entire Johnny Buck CD collection to charity!

At last, the engine was sputtering.

Music to my ears, Steven thought wearily. For the

first time in what seemed like a dozen miles, he dared to look up. No question, the mower had slowed way down. The fact that it was going up a hill didn't hurt either. After a moment, the tractor coasted gently to a stop. Steven took a deep breath and rolled off the hood onto the ground.

He stared up at Joe. "Don't tell me you found the brakes," he said sarcastically.

Joe wrinkled his brow as he stepped weakly off the mower. "Brakes?" he puffed. "Forget brakes. I think we're just plain out of gas."

Steven lay back. A wave of nausea swept over him. *If I never hear the words "riding mower" again,* he assured himself, *it will be too soon.* He lay as still as he could.

A door banged.

With a start, Steven sat up. His stomach was still churning. Turning around, he realized that the mower had stopped right outside the house where they had scared the twins out of their gourds the other day. He shaded his eyes and saw a woman walking quickly across the lawn.

"Oh, a riding mower," she called out enthusiastically.

Steven groaned.

The woman was standing above him. "You know, this is the strangest coincidence. The grass hasn't been cut since our gardener died." She kicked at a clump in front of her. "It's kind of shaggy, isn't it?"

Steven said nothing. He nodded his head a fraction of an inch—and felt dizzy all over again.

"I'm Mrs. Riccoli," the woman said. She extended her hand. "Could I offer you young gentlemen a job?"

"A job?" Steven perked up a little despite himself.

Joe straightened his shoulders. "You did say 'job,' didn't you?"

"That's exactly what I said," Mrs. Riccoli replied with a smile. "Our grounds actually extend pretty far back and could use a good bit of work. You can't see it from over here, but there's a shack that's completely overgrown with vines and weeds. We'd like to turn it into a gazebo or something if only we could *get* to it beneath the overgrowth. . . . Oh, goodness! I'm completely rambling. I don't even know if you boys are interested."

Swaying unsteadily, Steven stood up and took her hand. "Why, certainly, ma'am," he gasped grandly, trying not to throw up all over Mrs. Riccoli's shoes. Of course, mowing lawns was turning into one of his least favorite activities, but he knew an enterpreneurial opportunity when he saw one. "We at Wakefield and Howell would be very happy to have your business."

Even if I have to cut your grass with a fingernail clipper! he thought grimly, surveying the hulking mower in front of him.

Fourteen

I don't know if I can take any more of this, Jessica thought grimly, nibbling a fingernail. She was sitting on the couch in the Riccolis' living room on Friday night.

Next to her, Elizabeth looked up, startled. "What did you say?"

Jessica stared at her sister. Had she spoken aloud? "I didn't—say anything," she said hesitantly. "At least—I don't think so." :

Elizabeth didn't meet her gaze. "Yes, you did," she said. "At least—I thought you did."

Jessica took a deep breath. She could feel the muscles in her chest tighten. Upstairs, the kids were asleep. Peacefully, she hoped. But downstairs, she and Elizabeth were nervous wrecks. The ticking of the grandfather clock sounded louder than ever, and even the walls seemed to be closing in. *I don't want to spend another night in this horrible house,* she thought. *It's one nightmare after another—*

Elizabeth's head twitched. "What?"

"You're hearing things, Elizabeth," Jessica told her. The thought gave her the creeps. *Everything* was giving her the creeps tonight. If she looked hard at the spiral steps, she could almost see something descending the stairs. Something in a daisy nightgown. And one bunny slipper. And—

Jessica clamped her eyes shut. Just her imagination, of course.

Elizabeth sighed deeply. "I wish Mrs. Riccoli would hurry back," she said.

Almost without knowing what she was doing, Jessica stood up. "Come on," she said. "Let's go."

"Go?" Elizabeth asked. "Go where?"

Jessica seized her sister's hand and yanked hard. Elizabeth rose, as easy to pull as a rag doll. "To—" Jessica's voice suddenly felt thick. She swallowed hard. *To where?*

She didn't know.

"We're not leaving?" Elizabeth looked at her sister in bewilderment. "Mrs. Riccoli's not home, and we can't—"

"We're going to the secret room," Jessica said, cutting her sister off sharply. Her voice echoed off the walls: "room-room-oom."

The secret room. Numbly, Jessica caught her breath. Had she actually said that?

"To the secret room?" Elizabeth's eyes were wide. "But—"

"The secret room," Jessica repeated, walking with determined steps toward the spiral staircase.

She didn't really *want* to see that room. But somehow she felt she *had* to.

"This place gives me the creeps," Elizabeth whispered.

Jessica could only nod. The room was as still as a tomb.

"Why are we here?" Elizabeth asked in a hushed voice. She squeezed Jessica's hand.

"We're here to look for clues," Jessica whispered back.

"Clues?" Elizabeth repeated. "What sort of clues?"

"I don't know . . . just *clue* clues." Jessica tried to sound casual. "Anything that might help us figure out . . . what, you know . . ." Jessica swallowed hard. ". . . what the dreams and everything mean."

Jessica walked briskly to the bookshelf in the corner of the room. "Here," she whispered, running her finger along the old faded spines. "*Lamb and Pig Go to the Park. Busy, Busy, Beavers.*" She traced the letters on one especially worn-out volume. "*The Great Big Ball of String.* Have you ever read these books?" she demanded, turning halfway around toward her sister.

Elizabeth's face was a chalky white in the dim light. "No," she said softly. "But—but I've seen some of them before. In the—you know, in the library. They're, like, really old. Maybe twenty-five years old."

Jessica's finger stopped on a slim book with a torn pink cover. "*How Many Miles to Michigan?*" she said aloud, gently pulling the volume toward her. She drew in her breath. The title sounded familiar.

"It's a book of poems," Elizabeth said in a strangled voice. "'How many miles to Michigan?'" she quoted, leaning over her sister's back. "'Ride there 'ere you die—'" Her shoulders sagged. "I—I forget the rest."

"Mom had this book," Jessica said. With one finger she probed the edge of the cover. She felt a little dizzy. "She had it when, you know. When she was a kid."

"She still has it," Elizabeth said, as though trying to convince herself. "In the corner of the family room. On the bottom shelf."

Jessica didn't know why her heart was beating so furiously. With one hand she held the book in front of her. With the other she eased the cover open. Yellowed bits of paper floated to the ground. Jessica forced herself to look at the title page. A few words in faded blue ink leaped out to meet her eyes.

"This book is the property of Eva Sullivan," Jessica read aloud. Her heart returned to normal. She snapped the book shut, feeling a little better.

Elizabeth took a deep breath. "Well, of course it wasn't Mom's." She let out a forced laugh. "It was Eva's."

"Of course," Jessica echoed. Her eyes flicked around the walls. Over the bed hung a drawing of a very small girl with very big eyes, surrounded by a sea of empty space. It was signed "By Eva" in miniature orange and blue letters. Next to it was a black-and-white sketch of a little house that looked nothing like the Riccoli mansion. In front of it stood a man, a woman, and a tiny little girl. The man and the woman were smiling.

The little girl wasn't.

"How long—" Jessica's voice broke the silence. "How long do you think it's been since anyone was in here?"

"Years," Elizabeth breathed. "I don't get it, Jess. If the Riccolis knew the room was here, why haven't they carted all this stuff away?"

Jessica shook her head. Her eyes continued around the room. She was relieved to see there was no balcony door. *At least my dream hasn't come true,* she thought.

"What's in here?" Elizabeth pointed to a small door on one side of the room. "A closet?"

"A closet," Jessica assured her, trying to sound confident.

"You're going to open it?" Elizabeth raised her eyebrows.

Jessica realized that her hand had reached out to grasp the doorknob. She watched, dumbfounded, as her fingers twisted the knob and the door swung silently open. *It's as though I'm not in control of my hand,* she thought, blinking as dust floated out from the closet—

And then she gasped.

On the closet floor sat a bunny slipper.

Child's size.
Pink. With ears.
One slipper.
Only one.

One slipper. One thought resonated through Elizabeth's brain:
Then the dreams were real.
Slowly she backed away from the closet door, pulling her sister with her. She was dimly aware of silence all around her. She had never heard silence so absolute.

The twins stood in the center of the room, staring at the closet a few feet ahead of them. "Who *was* Eva Sullivan?" Elizabeth asked at last. "And what happened to her?"

Jessica only shook her head.

A gust of cold air swept suddenly through the room. Tensing her muscles, Elizabeth huddled into her sweatshirt. Just then, there was a loud bang behind her.

The door of the room had swung shut.

"The kids!" Elizabeth said, almost grateful for the interruption. "Come on, Jess, they'll hear it and wake up!" She sprang for the door, grabbed the handle and turned—

But the door wouldn't budge.

"Locked," Jessica whispered hoarsely, huddling near her sister to see.

Elizabeth gave the door an experimental push. It didn't move. She glanced at her sister, her blood running cold. "We're locked in a room that nobody even knows exists. . . ."

"If there's anywhere to slip the scissors in, I can't find it," Jessica said. It seemed as though hours had passed. She had poked along every inch of the door frame, trying to find a space to wedge Eva Sullivan's rusty old pair of scissors. "I can't find any weak spots in the door at all."

Elizabeth swallowed hard. "So what now?"

"If we kick really hard, maybe someone will hear us," Jessica said hopefully.

Elizabeth trembled. "It's a long way downstairs," she said. "And the door's pretty thick." She cleared her throat. "But Mrs. Riccoli will be home soon. And of course she'll come looking for us."

"Right," Jessica said in her firmest voice.

They stared at the heavy oak door.

"Do you smell something?" Elizabeth asked after a moment. She sniffed the air.

Jessica took a deep breath. *Smoke.* "A fire," she whispered.

"We're right above Andrew's room, I think," Elizabeth said. "That must be where the fire is. Did you check his room for matches?"

Jessica shook her head.

"Neither did I." Elizabeth stood all the way up. "The smell's getting stronger," she said in a shaky voice.

The two girls looked at each other. Then, as if

they were one person, they began beating their fists against the door and screaming.

"Let us out!" Jessica yelled at the top of her lungs.

"Olivia! Andrew!" Elizabeth cried.

"Wake up!" Jessica shouted. "Someone, anyone!"

"Save us!" Elizabeth screamed.

Jessica hardly dared to breathe. The fumes from the fire were unmistakable now. In a fury she banged her fists against the door, against the wall, against the floor. She wished one of the kids would wake up and come investigate. She wished—

"Help!" Elizabeth pleaded.

Jessica took a sideways glance at Elizabeth. Her face looked completely, totally, terribly pale. The air grew hotter, thicker, more stifling.

And no one was coming to help.

"Please!" Jessica wailed, raining heavy blows on the door.

But it didn't budge. Jessica clenched and unclenched her fists in terror. Sweat poured down her cheeks. Her lips felt like a block of wood. An anguished cry rose in Jessica's throat:

"Get us out of here before we die!"

And the sound echoed ominously off the walls:

"Die-die-die-"

The girl smiles as the flames rise higher. She sees them licking around the sleeping boy's bed, bright orange in the darkness. Orange with points of blue ...

Her smile grows wider. Orange and blue always were her favorite colors.

From above she can hear the screams of the two blond girls. The sound is music to her ears. *Louder*, she thinks, chuckling. *Louder.*

The slumbering boy tosses and turns. He mutters something in his sleep. The fire crackles and creeps toward his pillow. In the room above, the screams grow louder. The girl can hear the distant echo of fists against the heavy wooden door.

They got what they deserved, the girl thinks. *They should have listened to me. All of them.*

The flames burn brightly. A spark touches the boy's head. The girl lets forth an evil-sounding laugh.

Her promise, her wish, is about to come true. . . .

Created by FRANCINE PASCAL

Ask your bookseller for any titles you have missed. The Sweet Valley Twins series is published by Bantam Books.

SWEET VALLEY TWINS™

We hope you enjoyed reading this book. If you would like to receive further information about available titles in the Bantam series, just write to the address below, with your name and address:

KIM PRIOR
Bantam Books
61–63 Uxbridge Road
London W5 5SA

If you live in Australia or New Zealand and would like more information about the series, please write to:

SALLY PORTER
Transworld Publishers (Australia) Pty Ltd
15–25 Helles Avenue
Moorebank
NSW 2170
AUSTRALIA

KIRI MARTIN
Transworld Publishers (NZ) Ltd
3 William Pickering Drive
Albany
Auckland
NEW ZEALAND

All Transworld titles are available by post from:-
Bookservice by Post, PO Box 29
Douglas, Isle of Man, IM99 1BQ

Credit Cards accepted.
Please telephone 01624 675137 or fax 01624 670923
or Internet http://www.bookpost.co.uk
or e-mail: bookshop@enterprise.net for details.

Free postage and packing in the UK.
Overseas customers allow £1 per book (paperbacks)
and £3 per book (hardbacks)